I Aint Even Lyin

The lost art of southern story tellin

12-16-11

Scott Kelley

SCOTT KELLEY

authorHOUSE®

AuthorHouse™
1663 Liberty Drive
Bloomington, IN 47403
www.authorhouse.com
Phone: 1-800-839-8640

First published by AuthorHouse   11/04/2011

ISBN: 978-1-4670-3784-6 (sc)
ISBN: 978-1-4670-3783-9 (hc)
ISBN: 978-1-4670-3782-2 (ebk)

Library of Congress Control Number: 2011917611

Printed in the United States of America

Table of Contents

My Inspiration

Growin up in Northwest Florida as a young southern hillbilly boy, I loved huntin, fishin, and spendin time just ramblin through the woods, bays, and creeks. I have always loved the outdoors and just bein in the wild, wherever it carried me, was just fine by me.

When I was just a little runt, my family would spend weekends at my Grandpa Ed Lipham's farm, located just off Econfina Creek. Gettin to roam through those woods was a thrill to me, and I can even remember the smell of those woods after it rained. Grandpa had cows, hogs, and chickens and the old farmhouse was the first place I had ever stayed that had a fireplace. The only plumbing in the house was a spigot that put out just cold water and it only ran to the kitchen sink. Yep, he did have an outhouse and that was a rare thing in the 60's. I thought the outhouse was cool until the Florida heat kicked in. At night by the fireplace, my brother Mike and I would sit and listen to grandpa tell stories for hours on end. Grandpa loved to see our little imaginations take off on his adventures with him and that's when he nicknamed me "Peered Eye," cause my big ol' blue eyes would be fixed on him.

Take a little boy from a broken home and put him with a man that gave him the freedom to be a little boy and you have the makings of a happy ending. When I was about seven years old, Grandpa and Grandma moved a brand new, twice-wide, mobile home trailer to the farm. They put it just a little ways from the old farm house. I learned how to feed all the animals, milk the cows, and even churn some creamy butter. At night after supper, we would sit around shellin peas while grandpa told of his coon huntin adventures with his faithful hound dogs. He would tell us how things were when he was growin up. Every one of the stories he would tell would be plastered in my mind and the old farmhouse would always be in the background. He sure did have a way of captivating you with his stories. When it was bedtime and I was supposed to be sleeping, I would replay his many adventures over and over in my head. I sure did lose a lot of sleep because of Grandpa! I would love to have him here so I could learn more of the old ways and listen to his stories once again. I can't recall ever seein him mad or sad. I believe he knew he was blessed by the good Lord to be doin what he loved, bein a farmer. He's been gone for years now, but his stories live on in my imagination. My grandpa was a superhero in overalls!

My situation was a bit out of the ordinary as a youngster because I had 4 grandpas. My Papa Riley was a Pentecostal Preacher and he and Grandma Riley would visit often and spend the night with us. Papa would get up real early before daylight and make coffee. I can hear the spoon clankin in the cup still to this day, as he would stir in the milk and sugar. It would always wake me up and I would go on in there and have a cup with him. Mine was more milk and sugar than coffee, but I sure felt all growed up durin our mornins together. Sometimes I wonder if he was extra loud just to get me to come in there and talk with him. While we sat around the table waitin on my coffee to cool, Papa would tell me of his adventures as a hobo. (A hobo is someone who wanders around with no job or permanent home.) My Papa would catch trains and see the sights all over the United States. This life wasn't always the easiest for him, but he did have some good memories. He loved like he wasn't promised tomorrow and lived every other part of his life that way too. He sure was the type of man to tell you like it was and I learned from him that life is too short to hold it all in. His life was an example to me of the mercy of God and that you can't go too far that God doesn't know where you are!

I've been blessed to have another great man in my life, my Grandpa W.M. Pitts, Jr. He was a war hero that fought in World War II and lost his left arm as a very young man. When he came back home from the war, he didn't let his handicap stop him. He married my Grandma Elsie, had 5 kids and went into the heavy equipment business. His determination, kind words, and stories of growin up as a boy in the Bayou George area left an imprint on my life forever. He has a keen sense of humor and he always wears a smile on his face ready to give an encouraging word. I hope I can become half the man he is.

I had another grandpa that I didn't get the chance to know very well. My biological father, Mike Kelley, told me all about his father, C. B. Kelley. I learned that he was a jolly businessman in the Panama City area who died when I was in the second grade. He came to know God at a later age and became a very giving man who was well loved and remembered by many for his words of wisdom. I still live by many of the words he left to his family who imparted them to me.

The man that impacted my life the most is my daddy, Tommy Riley. He is one of the greatest men I know and I am the man I am today because of his godly example as a father. He raised me and my brother as his own after marryin our momma when we were just young boys. My momma died unexpectedly within a few short years of their marriage and he made the choice to keep us with him because of his love for us and our mother. God didn't stop there, a couple of years later, he also sent us a new godly mother, Deborah. At times, we were pressed down, but not destroyed; God truly does supply every need. I wouldn't trade this life for any other. My daddy took us fishin and huntin and we did all the things young boys loved to do. The thing about my upbringing that I appreciate the most was that my parents taught us how to be God-fearing men. I will forever be grateful for the unselfish acts of my parents, Tommy and Deborah; God used you to rescue me!

Above all, I want to thank Jesus Christ for His grace and mercy. He put breath into an infant boy and gave him life. He kept me through loss and didn't let bitterness take root. He gave me love from a man who had no obligation to me, except in his heart. He made sure my ears were filled with His Word. God could have decided that I was not worth a second or third chance after straying from my upbringing, living my life my way, and two divorces, but He is a God of many chances. At 30 years old, I returned to Jesus with nothing to offer Him. God can take nothing and make something out of it. I allowed faith to change my life and He was faithful to save my soul. He is the Master Carpenter and He rebuilt my life and gave me a new foundation. I have been married to my beautiful wife, Robin, for 17 years and we have 4 precious children together: Ariana, Tommy, Jonathan, and Alaya.

My passion to talk, talk, tell stories, talk, and write is very evident to those around me. The woods are my domain; when a tree can come to life, when a bird can talk, when the rustle of a leaf means I am being stalked; can you think of a better setting to let your imagination run wild? As you read, I challenge you to let your imagination do what it was intended to and bring it to life on paper.

The Run-Away Hearse

Back a few months ago I had one of the worst scares of my life. It all happened up near a town called Kinard. My long time huntin and fishin buddy, Randy Bevis and I, were out lookin for a big ol' coon track. Randy was a little bit late gettin out to the woods, so he met me on Road 12. I had just gotten back into coon huntin after bein out of the hound business awhile.

When Randy got to the bridge where I was waitin, we talked it over and decided to try to find some new places to hunt. We normally look for new huntin places in the daytime, but an exception was made this particular night. There were so many other hunters in our regular turnouts that we had to do somethin different.

An old road used to go on through to Kinard until years ago when a big ditch was dug across the road and a little bridge was built. The ol' bridge had been condemned for ages, but Randy and I decided to try drivin our small trucks across it anyhow. Randy's argument was since I weighed a few pounds less than him that I should go first and break the way.

My grandpa told me once that back in the late 1800s there was a lost community off in the woods near where we were huntin. I hadn't thought much about it until we were both on the other side. We drove on down to a fork in the road and found a huge coon track; I mean this was the "Papa Coon!"

We jumped out of our trucks and commenced to turn the dogs loose. We had three coonhounds: Smokey, Boss and Bo-Bo. The dogs started openin even before their feet hit the ground. They went straight in for a good, long ways until we could hardly hear them anymore.

I told Randy I was goin to ease around the corner to see if I could get a little closer. Randy went back to the fork and took the other road. Neither of the roads had been traveled in several years and both were pretty bad. I drove on up the road to an old wooden fence. The road went right up to what I made out as an old barn and stable. I stopped and listened to the dogs. When I got out of the truck and swung my light in the direction of the dogs, my heart just about stopped; there in the dark was a sight I'll never forget. It was a graveyard! Some of the biggest and most frightenin tombstones and crosses dotted the ground. It looked as if it was darker out there under the trees that filled the graveyard than it was where I was standin. Now, I ain't afraid of the boogieman or nothin, but this scenery did make my toes curl a bit. The sound of my dogs brought me back to reality and off Elm Street.

The dogs were headin in my direction pretty fast and I walked away from the truck to get lined up with them. Out of my peripheral vision, I could see somethin runnin through the graveyard. It was small and certainly not one of our dogs. Whatever it was though, it came right by me kickin up dust. It ran straight up a huge holler tree and into a big hole. I aimed my light on the tree and staring back at me was the biggest, bark-chewinest, boar coon I had ever seen. Within seconds, the dogs hit the tree with the coon's scent fresh in their nostrils. I was very proud to be the owner of these fine dogs.

About that time, I heard Randy hollerin on the C.B. He wanted to know what the hounds were doin. I told him they were treed and to come around to where I was. Just the sight and thought of that graveyard brought on one of those ideas that will put a giggle in your belly just thinkin about it. You know what I'm talkin about, the kind that you like to do to others, but not have done to you. I let my idea simmer a while; I wanted it to be a doozie.

In the meantime I walked on out to the tree to pet up the dogs. The tree was right behind an old wooden buildin covered with grapevines and such. Up against the tree in those same grapevines was the funniest lookin wagon I had ever seen. It had glass windows all away around it and there was a seat on top. The inside compartment was not high enough to sit in and it had a door not hardly big enough to crawl through.

The dogs were wearin themselves out jumpin on the tree and all, so I pulled them back and tied them to that old wagon. I could hear Randy buzzin down the road, so I had to do something fast if I was gonna pull one on him.

I walked to the back of the wagon and opened up the door. Just as I was closin the latch, Randy's lights peeped around the trees. I figured I could see every move he made as he walked out to the tree. When I was inside and settled, I realized why there wasn't enough room to sit up. A cold chill suddenly came upon me. You aren't supposed to be upright in this kind of wagon; it was a hearse wagon! I tried to open the door, no luck, so I tried again, but the door was stuck.

The dogs, which were tied to the front end of the wagon, were jumpin up and down at the ends of their ropes and not helpin at all. That wagon was shakin like a furless polar bear. I decided I would just calm down, lay back and wait for Randy to come lookin for me and then he'd get me out. When I laid back and tried to get relaxed, the things I felt underneath me pushed me to my limit. An old, stiff overcoat and a matchin top hat were draped across the remains of the latest member of the old community. I reckon this was a "dead end," cause he obviously didn't make it to the grave.

While my nightmare continued, Randy was about 30 yards from the tree and gettin kinda scared because I hadn't told him about the scenery, especially the creepy graveyard.

As my mind went back to all the scary stories I heard as a youngster, I finally couldn't take it anymore and I let out a blood-curdlin scream, which was the beginnin of a chain of events that made this the most memorable night of coon huntin Randy and I had ever had. When I hollered, the dogs went wild, Randy went wilder and I went wildest. Randy went back to the truck and called for the dogs, unaware that they were tied up. As he called the dogs, they dug their feet in the ground and tried to head his way. The dogs were carryin on so much that the coon just dove out of the tree and landed right in front of 'em. They broke the wagon loose from the vines and headed right after the coon, who ran in front of the trucks where Randy was. By this time, we were both the recipients of my mischievous trick.

The old wooden wagon wheels rolled like square tires. This mixed me and the bones all together. As the wagon rolled on and my breathin grew heavier, the windows got all fogged up. Randy had held back his fear as long as he could. All he could see was the hearse chasin three dogs through a graveyard. To make matters worse, when I turned on my light, all he could see was a form of somethin moving around inside it! Randy raised his automatic rifle and unloaded it at the wagon. I could hear bullets bouncin off the old tombstones. I knew that I would have to lay low and hug the bones or get myself shot. When I thought I might as well give up, the shootin finally stopped. I didn't hear anything from the dogs, and I didn't hear anything from Randy. Not knowin whether to yell, cry, or just be still for a minute, I decided to roll over and get out of this ol' box of bones. The sight before me was not a pretty one. Randy had gone and shot all three dogs and the wagon looked like a prop in an Al Pacino movie. Still shakin from the scariest experience of my life, I looked around for Randy. He was nowhere to be found and his truck had disappeared. When I made it to Randy's house, I had found his truck; it was on his front porch!

After I finally talked him into openin the door, Randy was fit to be tied. Once I explained ev'rythang and our blood pressure came down, we had a good laugh and a good story to tell our buddies. I saw a gleam in Randy's eyes that turned out to be the four gold teeth that hung in my clothes. We took them down to a pawnshop to see what they were worth and the ol' man down there gave us $1200.00 for them. With a $600.00 share of the money, Randy was ready for another adventure, but in the daytime and with a close eye on me!

They Walk Among Us

When I was twenty years old, I knew everythang; all you had to do was ask me. I hadn't long graduated from high school, uh, yes, I did graduate, and some thought I was quite the scholar. Once in the real world, gettin a job wasn't hard, but the work sure was. I.C. Contractors gave me a job workin construction in Picayune, Mississippi at the Sylva-Chem Corporation. I was just a laborer, but I enjoyed ev'ry bit of it; we poured concrete and even built a railroad bridge. Well, like all construction jobs, this one ended and I got laid off. I did have a pretty good chunk of change saved up so I decided that when I got home, I was goin to the river.

As soon as I pulled up to my own place, an acre and a third of land with a fine ol' singlewide house trailer sittin in the middle, I hooked up my boat right there in the driveway. I was goin catfishin for a few days. I loved campin on the side of the river; the thing I dreaded though, was the drive to Apalachicola. Drivin that far made me sleepy and when I get sleepy, I have been known to clip a guide wire on the side of the road or take out a mailbox or two. I'll admit it, I am a fall-asleep-at-the-wheel kind of guy.

The Break Away Lodge landin was a beautiful sight on the Apalachicola River. When I put my boat in the river that afternoon, it was straight up three o'clock. I had all my gear, tent, lantern, & of course, my ol' trusty Remington 22 Nylon 66 rifle. Like American Express, I never leave home without it. My catfish bait was near bout thawed in a bucket of water and I was rarin to go. It's always a great feelin for me to be gettin to the woods while the sun is still up. I have a mind sorta like MacGyver and I am prepared for anything. I have gotten out of many a pickle by havin a wire coat hanger or just an extra roll of toilet paper. Some folks don't mind me taken extra-long, but then again, they were the ones who benefitted most from the extra toilet paper.

Runnin up the river in my favorite rig, a 20hp Johnson on my 14' Kennedy Craft, was like goin to one of them head doctors, it was pure therapy. No worries, no stress, and no obligations—I had the world by the tail; it may have just been a tiger's tail that I had. Just about the time I ran under the train trussell, I remembered that no one knew where I was! Since I am a distant relative of He-man, it weren't me I was worried bout; it was momma. I had forgotten to call Momma and Daddy to let them know I was home from Mississippi and hadn't mentioned to nobody that I was goin catfishin for a few days. I knew I would get an ear full from Momma when I got home and bein I just used a whole box of Q-tips from the last time, I sure weren't lookin forward to anothern. Out of a litter of three, I am the one that didn't have to sleep on the porch, so I knowed she just worried bout me. I did lots of trompin through the woods after coon dogs, fishin, campin and many other crazy things, I reckon she figgered I would get bit or eaten by somethin.

As I traveled up the river, the smell of the wind in my face brought back memories of the many adventures I have had out here.

Campin, fishin and huntin with my daddy, brother and other crazy folks who wanted to come to paradise. Ah, those were the days!

I quickly got my camp set up in the mouth of the same slough we would always camp at when we were little boys. At 4:30, camp was set up, the fire was built, and for a redneck boy, I couldn't imagine nothin better. By dark: thirty, I had 23 bush hooks set and the grease a cracklin and poppin, cookin up three big swift water bream in my fryin pan caught right there at my camp. Why that sounded better than rain on a tin roof in the springtime. Man vs. Wild, if yer readin this, wipe your chin off, cause I know your mouth is a slobberin.

I cleaned up after a fine campin supper of fish, hushpuppies and sweet potato fries. I made sure to put everythang in its place and secure it well to keep the coons from wakin me up durin the night. The sky was clear with a million stars and a gentle, cool breeze. It's no wonder that the sandman won't come near me in this atmosphere. I'll tell ya, if a man could bottle this up, he'd sure have a thick wallet.

Anytime I was runnin the river at night, especially if I was by myself, I always wore my lifejacket. You never know what might be under the water or floatin downstream. So, I suited up and checked all 23 bush hooks. I had sixteen nice, big channel cats.

What a day!!! I got back to camp just fore midnight. The bank was kinda high and on a curve, the two reasons why Daddy always camped here. The wind blew down the river just right to keep you nice and cool and keep the skeeters away. The night sky was clear and the crackle of the fire was finally causin me to bog on down. No tent for me tonight, ain't nothin better than sleepin under the stars.

The next mornin, I checked the bush hooks early, got nineteen this time! I was usin an old secret recipe that I heard my buddy got from ol' Sim Taunton. He used cut bait mullet marinated in Aunt

Jemima's Butter Flavored Maple Syrup. If I heard that old secret recipe wrong, the catfish sure didn't know it, cause I already had more fish than I wanted to clean.

One of my biggest loves is to explore. I learned a lot from my grandpa, William Pitts Jr. Grandpa Pitts enjoys knockin around in the woods almost better than eatin. Well, maybe not quite that much, but he loves walkin through the woods seein what there is to see. This love of explorin comes in handy with me bein a hunter and fisherman and all. I have found some backwater nooks full of fish and some wood ridges covered with game. For just that reason, I have always liked Ingram Creek. It never fails that I catch at least one big ol' bream by a long abandoned sunken steamboat. I am often intrigued as to what caused it to settle to the bottom in Ingram Creek and the history behind it even bein there. I can't help but think of the old classic movie, The African Queen, because of the similarities.

Tippin along up Ingram Creek, if you want to get off the boat and on the hill, you had better pick a good spot since there are some places I believe you could sink up over your head in the mud. I just tipped along at a slow speed, lookin for a place to catch my eye. I don't know what exactly, but I'll know it when I see it. There it is, just up ahead, a wide waterway flowin into Ingram Creek.

The mouth of the little creek is covered up by a thick, wild scuppernong vine. For those of you who don't know, that's a wild grape vine and to those of us in the south, it's a scuplin. These suckers are good!! Once I get started eatin 'em, I can't stop. I don't feel so guilty eatin a honey bun after I've had a fill of those purple beauts.

Anyway, up that creek I went. After turnin in, I found that this little creek went way back into some tall virgin pine timber. Good thing they don't get much taller or else they would flip the world over. I eased on up about a quarter mile through the big ridge of pines and noticed some hardwoods beginnin to mix in. As I went a little further, the creek came to a dead end at a huge beaver dam. Time to explore!!! I tied up my boat and got out.

The beavers had themselves a nice dam built. The difference in the water level behind the dam and out in front was a good four foot. That's bout as big as I've ever seen. A lot of the underbrush and small trees were gone from the surroundin area as they had gone into buildin that elaborate and well-constructed dam.

Lookin for game sign, I saw lots of turkey feathers around. I have come to know that if there are turkeys around, so is everythang else. As I walked way up and around this beaver pond, I noticed many squirrels, found a deer horn with five points on one side, but what I didn't find was any shotgun shells. I've learned to look for things like that and when I don't find any, I know that means ain't nobody else been here much.

While lookin around, I noticed several half-buried, orange, clay turpentine cups. It had been many years since they had been used. As I walked on, I found another beaver dam above the first one. WOW! Lookin across to the other side of this dam, I could see an old logger's shack or a camp of some sort. With this area not bein far from the Apalachicola National Forest, these woods had all kinds of camps. This one was a little different though, in the fact that it was more log-cabinish rather than campish. I was dyin to go over and pilfer through the old camp, you know, like you do when you go through other people's junk at a garage sale, only better.

So I started across the beaver dam, it was a long ways and I knew I'd probably get wet. Just as I got almost all the way over, I came up on a spot in the dam where there was a little bit of water runnin over the top. It got kinda boggy and I was tryin to be careful. Then it happened! A hot coal of fire hit the back of my right calf.

I just didn't see him with everything else in the dam he blended in so well. A sure-nuff grown cottonmouth moccasin had branded me. Momma's nightmare was comin true; I was bit for the first time in all my galivantin by a snake. My split-second decision was to crawl the rest of the way to the old log camp. It was too far back across the dam, ev'ry bit of a hundred yards. I didn't know where the big moccasin had gone and my gun was back in the boat; all I had was my pocketknife. The cabin seemed like the best choice.

That snake sure pumped some venom in me cause the scorchin pain in my leg was affectin my ankle and my knee. I had to hurry and see if there was something I could use in or around the old cabin. I saw some big claw marks as I checked the windows. Not real comfortin, even if you are dyin from a snakebite. You could plainly see that the shutters had been peeled off the windows. Pushin past the heebie jeebies in my belly, I peeked in the window and at first glance, I could tell this place was way too old to have a first aid kit layin around. I staggered around to the front door only to see the front door had been clawed off, too.

Out back, behind the cabin, was an old smokehouse. I could see where the salt had been, beins this was the only place where the ground was disturbed. Wild animals of all kinds will lick the salt from up under the salt room. As I managed to get around to the back of the smoke house, the effects of the snakebite became more intense. I was sweatin in a strange way; this was becomin very serious. As I was draggin my fingers through the claw marks on the smoke house wall, it became apparent to me what had torn up the cabin and the smoke house.

Somethin moved under my foot. A loud clank, a loud snap and a blood-curdlin scream that sounded like it came from a girl! The largest steel trap I have ever laid my eyes on, nearly four feet long, had sprung shut on my poor ol' right leg. The snap was the sound of my bone crackin. I screamed again and it echoed through the tops of those tall trees, you could have heard it for miles. It hurt so bad, I forgot about the snakebite. All I could do at this point was pray for a miracle and make sure there wasn't anything wrong between God and me.

All kinds of things were runnin through my mind. Bears had obviously been here some time in the past. I couldn't go anywhere and right here beside the beaver pond, a gator would find me for sure. Nobody knew where I was, so nobody was gonna be lookin for me. I hollered 'til I was hoarse and the pain had numbed a bit.

Surprised that I was still alive, it was ironic that the bear trap was above the snakebite. Lookin back now, that trap probably slowed the flow of the venom, somewhat prolongin my life. The trap was old and huge and I couldn't squeeze the springs apart to save my life. Even with the anchor chain rusted in two from the big piece of iron stickin out of the ground, I still weren't goin nowhere. I was weak and the trap was too heavy. I know you're thinkin that a normal man would be dead already. It was late afternoon and my life was nearin an end. My biggest worry at this point was would anyone find me dead, much less alive.

As I began to drift in and out, I could hear somethin comin out in front of me but I couldn't see anythang. I started wonderin if it was just all in my head and there really was nothin there. I kept hearin somethin over my shoulder and as I tried to see, it reminded me of one of those blurry pictures you're supposed to stare at 'til a picture appears. I mostly just see the blur on those things. Then I saw him. The scariest part was the gold eyes with the black pupils peerin out of the darkness over my shoulder. I have to tell you, I was scared to death, but, ya gotta know if you were in my shoes, it had been a bad day already.

It wasn't a bear, a gator, or the venom playin tricks in my head. It stared at me, not blinkin, as if in a standoff. At one point, I figgered he was tryin to decide if I was worth eatin or not. So, with my last bit of strength, I decided to do what I do best, I started talkin to it. Those of you who know me, I know you're surprised. Maybe it was the venom, but I don't know now what I even said to him. It must've worked.

It bent down and picked me up and those eyes seemed to really show a concern for me. Whatever it was, he had no problem pickin my 160 lb. self right up. He was holdin me so gently; I didn't even try to fight to get out of its hands. The most puzzlin thing that I struggled with, was that as he passed through the last gleams of light, I could see the long brown hair coverin him. He walked up tall, like a man. His eyes still glowed in the dark, but I couldn't figger out what he was. I stayed awake for about another five minutes or so and the last thing I remember was goin up the side of a high oak ridge on the backside of the beaver dam, then it was black.

In and out of consciousness for what must have been a few days, I woke up to what I thought was a house, though nothin like I'd ever seen before. There were six or eight of the creatures and they were tendin to me steadily. They were all covered in hair, mostly brown but different shades. Some of them were bigger than others. I am just gonna come out and tell ya my conclusion, I was in the house of Bigfoot. I hate to even tell you that name, cause I know some of you may think I was delusional. All I know for sure is that I woke up and was in their house, pen or whatever you wanna call it. They had a couple of lamps sittin around with a beautiful glow and they put out enough light to see very well with no outside light comin in.

The bear trap was off and my leg felt funny when I saw it for the first time on the hard concrete lookin floor. I just knew they had sawed it off at my knee. I gasped and all the attention was on me. As I looked a little more, my britches were cut off at the knee and my leg was buried down in a hole in the floor. They had black mud packed all up around my leg. I figgered that was all right as I remembered a story my Grandpa Lipham had told me as a young boy about a man who had been rattlesnake bit. The man had been out huntin and on his way home, cut through a big ol' palmetto flat. Just as he was nearin his house, he got bit by a rattlesnake. He told his family he'd be back in a couple of days after he was well. He went down by their waterin spring, buried his leg in the sour, stinkin black mud and sat a spell. He was back at the house, just like he said, in a couple of days with just two little sore spots where the fangs had punctured his leg.

As I got my senses back, I figgered out there were only two of the creatures that were takin care of me. There was Big Maw, that's what I called her, and a young male about three quarters grown that I called Brown. He was the one that had rescued me and brought me to their house.

Bigfoot. The name doesn't even come close to explainin the vast knowledge and understandin they have. The way they tie in to the chain of life in our area will really blow most of y'all's minds.

Their houses were constructed similar to a beaver dam but on so much more of a grander scale with several connectin rooms. The floors main structure and support is Juniper logs for strength and flotation. When Juniper logs are dried, they will float higher in the water than any other timber we have available in this area and are slower to decay and rot. Next, the logs are covered with a mixture of twigs, sap and clay to make a "swampcrete" floor. Each room has a dome ceiling also plastered with swampcrete. They used taller and bigger trees to create the dome, and then layered with smaller and smaller trees, limbs and right on down to the leaves. The ceilin was tied right into the floor in each room using the swampcrete like spacklin.

Their houses floated. They would rise and fall with the water level of the river. Part of the home is situated out over the edge of the beaver pond with an entrance and exit into the beaver pond. There are several trap door entrances and openins through hollow trees all over the top of the house. The house was built around trees that acted as an anchor and kept it from driftin around. When the water would rise, so would their house. It was genius and interestin because what made it functional, disguised it as well. When the house floated up, it appeared to be one of those high water knolls or ridges covered in leaves and small vegetation. Thinkin back over the beaver ponds I've seen, here and all over, it makes me wonder how long they've been among us and how many I have ever tromped right over without even knowin.

These creatures are smarter than I originally thought. They first reminded me of hairy Indians. As I sat there watchin, while my leg was healin, I began to be aware of what was goin on. The menu consisted of dried meats, herbs, nuts, raw vegetables and even some things that I have no clue about. They are very organized and clean with all types of herbs and dried things stored in swampcrete pots. Unlike civilized pottery, swampcrete will not break, even when dropped. Many of the swampcrete pots had ointments made of natural minerals and plants out of the river and swamp.

Big Maw herself took care of my snakebite. She drained it and doctored it ev'ryday. I don't know what she mixed in that mud, but it was some stankin stuff! It worked though, whatever it was. While she was workin on me, Brown stared. He watched ev'ry move I made and listened to ev'ry word I said. It's a wonder he got any sleep at all! It was as if he wanted to learn what I was sayin cause I talked to them all the time. Course they never talked back, but at least they didn't complain. Well, the others paid me no mind; I figured if they could talk, those would be the ones to ask me to hush.

After my snakebite healed, Big Maw and Brown snatched and pulled my broke bones to set it back up right. I didn't cry out but the tears sure poured down my face. When Big Maw saw that, Bigfoot that she was, she showed compassion when she wiped the tears off my face. You can't hold it back when broken bones are set two or three weeks after a break. Brown took over then and tied splints around my leg and Big Maw covered it in, you guessed it, swampcrete for my own custom-made Bigfoot cast. That swampcrete was a true medical marvel in the wilderness.

At this point, I was able to hobble around and they gave me free run of their home. I was always taught to respect someone else's home and acted accordingly. Even the others were beginnin to warm up to me.

I finally got to go out of the house with Brown. With the direction of hand signals and a type of sign language, he led me to a shaded area and showed me why we don't see them anymore than we do. Wow! Once in the shade and the shadows of darkness, the Bigfoot disappeared. As I write this, words will not and cannot do justice to the really amazin cloakin and camouflagin abilities they have.

I have always been fascinated by animals; I even did a paper in school about polar bears. Before you ask what this has to do with the Bigfoot, just let me tell ya. The polar bear's hair is not white, it is transparent. It is white because of the reflection off the snow and ice. The Bigfoot also has transparent hair, but with an added ability. The difference is the Bigfoot have a chameleon ability to blend in to their surroundins. Just like the lizard, they can change the color of their hair to match their environment. Unless you can catch them in direct sunlight, you will never know they are there. Brown, my newfound friend, even smiled when he saw how impressed I was with his camouflagin ability. There's no tellin how many Bigfoot we've walked right by and never even had a clue.

In the full three moons that I stayed with this tribe of Bigfoot, I saw many amazin thangs. I'll tell you a few of them that completely changed the way I look at wildlife and its effects on the Bigfoot. The beaver probably has the biggest relationship to the Bigfoot. If there are beavers around, there's gonna be a Bigfoot in most cases. Beavers are a breathin chainsaw and the Bigfoot utilizes this to their benefit. I watched Brown, with my own eyes, rub a mixture of herbs and sap on the base of some trees he wanted cut down. Within a week, there were six large and eight small limbless trees on the ground. In turn, the Bigfoot will not let a gator in the beaver pond. I ate a lot of gator and big loggerhead snappin turtles while stayin with the tribe. The Bigfoot security company protected the breathin chainsaw family.

I remember one time, the biggest Bigfoot, I just fondly called him Hulk, brought two gators in to the prep room. That was where they did all the fixin, preparin and tendin to stuff. The gators were eight and eleven feet. Hulk had killed them with his bare hands. He was an impressive hunter and even though he didn't know what I was sayin, he knew I was braggin on him. He even got to struttin around, you know, how a feller will do when he's right proud of himself. Oh, and let me just tell you, Gator Jerky with the Bigfoot all natural rub and seasonin, is some very good stuff!

The river went up in the first part of November a good bit, must've rose about ten or twelve feet, floodin the swamp. The house just floated up. You could hear hogs and deer on top of the roof. From the river, it would have just looked like a high spot of land. No tellin how many high ridges I've seen over the years and, who knows, all of them may have been floatin Bigfoot houses. One time I got to see what the trap doors were all about. Hulk stood under it, reached through, and in one swoop pulled down through the ceiling, a huge ten-point buck. He bare handedly broke his neck with ease; if only my daddy had taught me to hunt like that!

Big Maw carried Brown and me with her to a place in the swamp that was full of preacher pulpits. Now don't go mistaken that for the church kind. The kind I'm talkin bout are a type of plant belongin to the Venus flytrap family. It is mostly green and has a long funnel that flies and other insects go into and then can't get out of. This trip to find the preachers pulpits had ev'rythang to do with the right time of the year. Have you ever wondered where the lightnin bugs go? Well, I'll tell ya, there ain't enough redneck youngun's runnin around makin redneck flashlights to explain their decline; not to mention, it's too hard to catch enough to fill up a mason jar. I did hear tell of a bee-keepin feller that crossed his honeybees with the lightnin bugs so they could work at night and bring up his honey production. However, I wonder about the valididity of that story and also if it's true or not.

Big Maw had us out there for a week in that swamp just before the preacher's pulpits started dyin off, collectin lightnin bugs out of them plants. The funnels were full of 'em, most were still alive too. Big Maw took the bugs, mixed them with some secret concoction of herbs and tree saps, and then put the mix in the swampcrete pots. When you took the lid off, it created the beautiful glowin lamps in the Bigfoot den. Once uncovered, the lamps would glow nearly twelve hours.

I studied ev'rythang they did the first month, with a kind of wary eye. This tribe is a tribe of thinkers with a lot of animal in them, but definitely not in the ape family. As my healin continued, by the second month, I felt the mutual trust and I even felt like a part of their family. By the end of third month, I knew it was nearin time to go and they knew it, too. The last night with them felt like a real family gatherin. We ate good, I talked, and they listened. Maybe they understood. I hugged Big Maw and she just patted my head. The next mornin, Hulk and Brown took me to where they had my boat hid out.

I am so blessed that they were there to save my life and that they did it even at the risk of exposin theirs. I realize my time with the Bigfoot family was not a tradeoff for them to learn from me about my world. That would not have impressed them much, cause they have been watchin us for years. I do hope they saw somethin in me that would help them realize that not all of us are bad. I go back from time to time and wonder if they know the sound of my walk. Am I walkin across one of their rooms? I realize even now that there is Bigfoot among us in the woods and river swamps. The three months I spent with the Bigfoot changed the way I look at things. They saved my life when they didn't have to and educated me to the fact that there is no place for laziness. Everyone plays a part and has a job to do.

I will have to say, when I got back home, my momma was relieved and peeved to see me. Is it possible for someone to be both at the same time? I just told her that I was with a Bigfoot family campin out in the river swamp. Of course, she didn't believe me, and I don't suppose you do either!

Bigger Than the Biggest

Ever since I was a very young boy, I loved to go off fishin with my daddy, Tommy Riley. He was always prepared with whatever kind of bait it would take to catch any kind of fish. It didn't matter if we were fishin in lakes, ponds, creeks or rivers around our area. Whether it was bream, bass or shell cracker, we would load the boat. When you catch so many fish that your cow milkin muscle is to sore to move your arm, you know you have caught some fish. Smellin them out like hounds, we would search out shell cracker beds in March and April. In May and June, we'd find the bream beds. Bass fishin was always included on ev'ry trip, but we never went just bass fishin.

My daddy didn't have any of them high fallutin Ambassador 5000 bait castin rod 'n reels. We mostly used the best rod n' reel combo ever made, that's right, the Zebco 33. My brother Michael and me was taught as little boys how to cast accurately. I am a professional Zebco 33 fishin wrangler and I have caught several eight to ten pound bass on a good ol' Zebco. I wish I had my own fishin show and could fish for all kinds of big game fish, usin only the Zebco 33. I can see it now . . . Presenting, Scott Kelley, World Renowned Fisherman and Champion, reelin in a big ol' sail fish on a, what? It can't be, oh! But it is . . . a ZEBCO 33!! I would prove to the world that once again, it is the best all-around fishin combo, and, no bird nests included! (By the way, a bird nest is what you get when the reel spools out too much line too fast and gets all tangled up when you are usin an expensive bait-castin reel.) The Zebco 33 is about 1/10th the cost of one of the expensive bait casters. So you do have to be sure and keep it oiled and in good workin condition, specially on the drag.

In August of 2010, we were fishin in a lake in the Panama City, Florida area known as Deerpoint Lake. Deerpoint Lake is a dammed up body of water that feeds the county water supply from the many creeks that flow into it. When Deerpoint Lake comes up in a fisherman's conversation, well, you will get some that say they hate it and some that say they love it. The key to likin it is you just have to learn how to fish it. I know this lake like the back of my hand as I was raised up sleepin in the bow of my daddy's boat many a night. I learned how to drink black coffee while fishin on this lake cause our fishin trip generally lasted longer than the one cold drank that I brought with me. FYI: Yoo Hoo was my favorite. I learned to eat wigglers cause, well, ok, I didn't ever eat the bait, that's just yucky.

My uncle, Mike Pitts, is probably one of the best bass anglers that ever came from these here parts. He has won lots of money and boats in tournaments. I went fishin with him in the early years in a little ol' jon boat, and more recently, in a very fine bass boat. Either way, he is a bass catchin machine. He don't know how to use a Zebco and don't know much about a bird nest on his fine reels.

Well, I'm bout to bust waitin to tell you the most unbelievable story of a once in a lifetime fishin trip that happened on that August outin. Uncle Mike knows how much I enjoy fishin Deerpoint, so he clued me in to a backwater lake that he knew of. You have to go way up the Kline's cutoff where it runs out into the stumps close to Econfina Creek. There is a tall bald palm with an active Osprey nest in it and when you get to that tree, you go due west through the stumps and lily pads to the shoreline. There will be what looks like a cypress swamp. If you look closely, you can navigate through the trees. In a small boat, you'll have to pole, paddle and scrape your way into a five-acre flowin spring pond. He said, and I don't know the proper terminology, that your boat will slowly drift counter clockwise around the whole pond, kinda like a whirlpool. The edges have a little grass with several deep open springs boilin up.

Me, my oldest daughter, Ariana, who is fifteen years old, and my oldest son, Tommy (AKA Crockett), who is eleven years old, and a couple of friends, Kerry and Brandon, finally got our chance to go up and try to navigate our way into this pond. We could tell no one had been in there fer years. I actually had to break down an old rotten duck blind to get the boat out on the main body of water. Once we busted through the blind, we ran into one of those issues that you know you will eventually have to deal with.

As the old duck blind collapsed, two big moccasins hit the water and took off. Yes, they were big and no, I didn't see em til they hit the water. Thank goodness they didn't land in our boat. These two snakes took off across the top of the water and of course, I was studyin them intently as I am not much of a snake person. To me, all snakes are deadly. Well, the two moccasins moved on across the pond toward a toppled down cypress tree lyin right on top of the water. Just as the biggest one got close to the tree, a bass with the head the size of a five-gallon water bucket exploded out of the water knockin the snake up in the air. I was speechless! Imagine that. What I had just seen, well, that don't happen every day. I told the young'uns, "You two have just witnessed a monster bass try to take out a huge moccasin." That is the first time I ever seen anythang like that.

I was scramblin around in my boat, lookin fer somethin, but not knowin exactly what. Bill Dance or even ol' Red Hollerin had never showed viewers what to do in a situation like this. The way I figger it, if we presented the right bait out across that hole in front of the fallen tree top, we might get a shot at catchin the hugantic bass. This fish really shook me up, so in all the lookin through my tackle box and under the bow of the boat, all I saw that remotely resembled the big moccasin, was my gas line. That was the closest thing to the snake in size, length and color.

I know it sounds crazy, but at this point, I was excited that my kids were so excited. I was willin to try anythang and unhooked my gas line from the tank. I figured that the worst thing that could happen was that I'd half to paddle. We got to work quickly, picked out the best pole in the boat, Crockett's Ugly Stik, rounded up the newest of our Zebco 33's and rigged it up. We put five hooks down the gas line usin some black zip ties and tied it into the fishin line.

We all agreed that I would cast and try to tease the monster bass out of hidin with the gas-line snake. Whatever happened, we would be prepared to help each other in whatever way we could. I nervously cast the homemade snake lure across the end of the treetop, just over to the backside of the fishin hole. I hit the button to stop the line right at the edge. Then, slowly workin the floatin gas hose, I snaked it across the open hole and right by the top of the tree. Not goin very far at all, it was plain to see him charge as he made a wake like a torpedo headed for his target. Our full attention was on this fish, we knew it was him.

The huge lunker bass hit the hose and just as I hesitated my retrieve, his large head came fully out of the water and he hit the hose at the back end. I could see he had over one half of the hose in his mouth. As he went under, I quickly hit the button on the Zebco 33 and thumbed the drag to make sure it was free enough. It would be smarter to tighten it after the fish was on than for it to be too tight and break em off. You know, I never claimed to be any better at bass fishin than anybody else, but I knew this fish was bigger than most of the legendary bass fishermen ever seen.

Counting out loud to myself . . . one, two, three, four, five, I made sure I gave this hungry hawg enough time to take the bait. Then I quickly reeled the line tight. I held the line against the pole and set the hook hard. I could not believe what happened next. The pole doubled over, puttin Tommy's Ugly Stick to the test. I tightened the drag to just the right adjustment, started reelin and pumpin this once in a lifetime bass to the surface. I called Ariana to take the pole. She was takin her time tryin to get the fish to the boat. Tommy's job was to help maneuver the boat and help coach his sister on landin the giant. My job was to do whatever I could to get my hands on this monster bass and get him in the boat.

The spring pond was showin its depth while the big bass steadily dove down on his first run. Ariana was doin an outstandin job workin the fish, pumpin and reelin and reelin and pumpin. We were workin as a team. Tommy had a paddle in his hand and was keepin the line from gettin tangled in the trollin motor and keepin it free from any snags. I was so proud to see the focus of brother and sister workin together on this fishin adventure of a lifetime.

Our team was finally gainin ground. After about five minutes of back and forth, of reelin a lot of line in, then the big fish takin it out again, all of a sudden, it was as if he just gave up. The water was very clear and we could see the bass at what we guessed to be about twenty feet down. We were really expectin him to try and make another run, but were hopin we could get him to the surface first. Ev'rythang was in place but a dip net. Ours hadn't been used in so long, it had dry rotted. We would have to improvise again.

As the big largemouth bass got closer to the top, we could see more and more how big he really was. When his head finally broke the top of the water, with half of the gas hose hangin out of the side of his mouth, we could tell there wasn't much fight left. I didn't no more get out of my mouth, "Man, what a fish!!", 'fore ol' Crockett bailed off the boat. He wrapped himself around that fish like a bun around a hot dog. I knew Crockett had the death grip on our fish and wasn't gonna let em go.

Ariana grabbed the gas line, I grabbed Crocket by the shirt and Crocket hollered out, "Forget me, grab the fish!" With one hand on his bottom lip and one hand under his gills, I drug the biggest bass anyone of us had ever seen into the boat. I was hoopin and hollerin as I pulled ol' Crocket in the boat and Ariana was holdin that Ugly Stik in the air like a gladiator who'd just won a battle. The Zebco 33, America's best all-around reel, had performed well and done its job again, just as I expected it would.

Wow, what a fish! He wouldn't fit into the live well; it wasn't built for a fish of this size. Sorry folks, but this biggun wasn't goin back in the water like one of those catch and release deals the boys on TV do. Out of the ice chest came the snacks and the drinks to make room for this feller. He was truly the biggest bass I ever laid my eyes on. I never really imagined a bass could get this big. I don't reckon I ever heard a fisherman use the words "I've got an ice chest full of one fish!" We even had to take out some of the ice to fit him in there. He really filled er up. We couldn't keep the lid closed; one would open it and look, then close it up, only for the rest of us to wanna take a peek.

What a beautiful fish this bass was, the markins he had were just what you would expect to find on a clear water fish. He was dark on the top, but lightened up down the sides with beautiful greens and golds and sported the black bass markins that truly made this bass the total package.

After all the action died down, I looked around for our fellow fishin buddies, Kerry Newell and Brandon Schrier, who were about thirty yards away in Kerry's boat. I hollered out, "Did y'all see that?" Brandon held up his camera and said, "Not only did we see it, we got pictures!" Kerry had follered right behind us into the pond and started riggin his poles. When the action started, I had completely zoned out ev'rything around me. I had assessed our assets and the components on hand to solve problems, just like I learned to do in the Navy Seals. We were taught to improvise with materials on hand to accomplish a successful mission.

We finally got to my daddy's house where we could weigh the fish, get our hugs, high fives and pats on the back. I couldn't wait to get this giant bass on the scales. My daddy was a proud grandfather as I told the story of the one that finally didn't get away. Daddy's old Piggly Wiggly produce scales showed our fish to weigh twenty-three pounds and eleven ounces.

Thanks to Kerry's smart phone, we knew the world record was twenty-two pounds and four ounces, which was caught around fifty years ago. World Record? World Record! my brain was exhausted. I still hooped 'n hollered a second time with Ariana, Ms. Purdy as I call her. Crockett and Paw-Paw were huggin and screamin that we had the coveted world record bass!

The very next morning, we were down at the Game and Fish Commission Office to get weighed in. We were so excited as we told the story in detail again. Lookin back now, I remembered the moment in our story when the brows were raised. With the scales out, the official weight was recorded at twenty-three pounds and five ounces, a full one-pound and one ounce larger than the world record. This is the new world record, the biologist told me, but there is the gas poisonin issue. As he was takin swabs of the gill area, he told me that he couldn't officially give us the record until the tests came back. Right then, I knew what was about to happen.

I went to the ice chest, closed the lid, picked it up and told my kids to come on, we had to go. The biologist's last words as he followed us to my truck, was that he would like us to leave the fish with him for further testin. I never said a word. If they were gonna take the world record from my kids, they weren't gonna keep the fish, too.

I've thought it all over and it wasn't intentional, but never would I have thought that we would catch a fish on our gas line and the world record bass would squeeze the pump bulb and inject himself with gas! Still, to myself, Ms. Purdy and Crockett, August 27, 2010 will go down as the day we caught the World Record Bass and we have the fish to prove it.

Bush Hookin Can Be Unhealthy

I love spendin time with my family. I feel my job is to teach my boys manly, "sandhillbilly" culture. We've heard that this is a dog-eat-dog world and bein I don't eat dog, I figure huntin and fishin for wild critters is what we're gonna do. We'll save "Rover" for sure-nuff hard times.

The wild Choctawhatchee River, with all its snags and stumps is one river I love to spend time on. It's also convenient; I can get there from my house in about 30 minutes. Campin on the side of that river just opens the eyes of my 2 boys, Tommy and Jonathan. Tommy is 11 and we call him "Crockett" after who else but ol' Davy. Jonathan is just a little feller of 7 years and his hero has always been Dan'l Boone, so it's just fittin that we call him "Boone." Somethin about the sound of movin water, the dark night, and those big owls talkin back and forth just brings on the anticipation of excitement and adventure. All these ingredients tend to keep my boys close to the glow of the fire. Out on that river at night fills a young boy with all kinda boogieman thoughts and it'll make him listen to his daddy's instructions better too.

On August 12, 2010, we maneuvered through all the turns and bends in my faithful 14' Scandy White aluminum boat, headin once again to my favorite spot on the river. We have a routine when we set up camp and tonight was no exception, so we set out to get 'er done. In Squirrel Slough, the crackle of the fire was nice that Friday evenin, specially after a long hectic week at work. Crockett and Boone were laughin and hollerin as they chased, stomped, and of course, got wet and muddy. The sound of them two boys, just bein boys, was a kinda therapy to my ears. We had a great night that evenin just roastin hot dogs over the campfire on a "special stick" that Boone cut for each of us with his very own pocketknife.

Some things have become habit for us. For instance, on any waterway, we wear life jackets; I've heard so many horror stories of accidents that could have been avoided by just takin the time to wear one. I also play a game with the boys, especially Crockett, it's like a "what-if this happened" game. A kid can't possibly experience ev'rythang that could happen, so I think preparin for as many "what-ifs" is my job as their daddy. I've taught Crockett how to crank, operate, and stick-steer the 40 HP Honda motor. He likes that kind of grown-up stuff and seems to take pleasure in bein seen by the passin boats. I reckon I was that way too, cause I couldn't wait to grow up neither. I spent lots of time lookin for opportunities to prove I was a man, which meant less time lookin where I was goin. Who put that wall there?

Swift water, two brothers learnin to work together and a wasp nest half the size of a dinner plate makes for memories not soon forgotten! Some cars can go from 0 to 60 in a few seconds, well, so can my two boys when you stir up a wasp nest. Teamwork turns into, "I hope I can run faster than you." Relaxation turns into evacuation and ev'rythang is turned upside down. It's not like you don't know what's about to happen now, but I'll tell ya anyways. I chose an ol' cedar to tie up to, but before I could get the rope around it, the current started pullin the boat. I proceeded to paddle back when the paddle hit an overhead limb. While all of this is happenin, Crockett is checkin the last hook. Just like a meteor fallin from the sky, the huge wasp nest landed in front of his face. We come to find out that they were a mite unfriendly bunch; they just didn't seem to have a lot of southern hospitality. Well, wouldn't you be upset too if your home went from a treehouse to a houseboat? Boone didn't waste any time, he took off like a flash of lightnin, completely ran out of boat and got away with a splash. Unfortunately, Crockett wasn't as lucky; he had a front row seat to all the action. In all the commotion, Tommy had managed to hook himself with the last bush hook. Ol' Crockett was a flouncin 'round like a fish and at the same time wrappin the line around his body like a mummy. Those wasps worked him over, bein as he was in a "bind" and all. As I ran onto the bow of the boat to help Crockett, I had somehow forgotten what a Wood Wasp sting felt like. It only takes one sting to refresh your memory. One hit me smack dab on the forehead, which was doubly bad for me cause not only did it hurt like fire, but it also gave my wife a target to aim for. "Like a good father, Scott Kelley's there," and pushin past my pain and through the wild beasts, in one swift motion I cut the line to the bush hook with one hand and reached into the water to pull Boone back into the boat with the other. The Karate Kid would have been jealous! Just as quickly as it had begun, it had ended. Because of the ruckus, I never managed to get the rope around the tree and the river current continued to pull the boat safely away from the swarm. My daughter, Ariana, says I should try to think more like "Pollyanna" and find a reason to be glad. So, here goes: By midnight we had "braggin rights" to 33 of the prettiest channel and blue catfish you ever did see; a story no one would believe without pictures; and for my boys, another memory of their heroic father riskin life or limb for his sons. Last, but not least, our biggest catch of the night weighed in at a whoppin 82 pounds! Ol' Crockett got caught by our last hook right through his booger-pickin finger. Poor fella, he is in a mess now cause he has some of the biggest boogers I ever did see.

Back out in the main flow of the river, we assessed the finger damage and caught our breath. After a thorough examination, I concluded that the hook went clean through Crockett's index finger. Since I am somewhat-of-a-doctor, this was a piece of cake. I tied off to a stump in the middle of the river bend, broke off a stick, stuck it side-ways in his mouth and told him to bite down. At the ripe old age of 11, I could tell Crockett was taking a couple more steps toward manhood and with no tears or words, he faced it like a man. Out of my tackle box, I grabbed the very needle nose pliers my daddy had given to me as a boy and there ain't no tellin how much of my DNA was on them bad boys. Snap! That's the sound the hook made as the sharp jaws of the pliers ruined a good hook. Off comes the barb and out slides the hook. Boone looked at me and said, "You ARE just like a doctor!" I could not let the little man be confused and I confirmed his suspicions. What a night it turned out to be! A mishap turned into a learnin lesson that my boys will never forget and what don't kill ya makes ya stronger. As we made our way back down river toward the camp, Boone snuggled up at my feet fast asleep and the cool wind feelin wonderful on my face, I couldn't help but have an overwhelmin feelin of joy. This is what life is about and would it be worth living if you couldn't live the next day with hope that it would be better than the day before? I did take note that Crockett held the Q-beam spotlight intently with eyes forward, a little more focused on each snag and bend in the river. Now Tommy will have a better tomorrow because he has hope that it won't have wasps or finger-attractin bush hooks in it.

Back at the camp, 'round the warm fire, the first aid kit gets a good workout and we all drift off to sleep on that perfect, well, near-perfect August night. We are bone-tired and pay no attention to the echo of the owls as they tell of the night, like they always do.

I automatically woke up early, cause that's what I've always done, most specially on weekends, cause it's my time and I want to get as much adventure out of it as I can. Rousin the boys, on the other hand, was a job that even Rambo wouldn't apply for and the Benadryl didn't make it any easier. With my "mission" accomplished, I rewarded myself with a nice hot cup of camp coffee. The boys also enjoyed a beverage of chocolate milk as I slaved over their breakfast of pecan swirls. Thank goodness for gas stations is all I can say. We make our last minute preparations to check our bush hooks for the last time and head out for another adventure.

There is a lot that I do that is figured into my life because I have kids. Whether it's huntin, fishin, or just explorin, I try to bring it down to their level. It's got to be interestin and that's why bush hookin or trout linin is fun for kids. You and the kids go set the lines, then leave and come back and check on 'em later. You can do other things at the camp while you are waitin. The possibility of catchin a monster is always in the back of my mind. I guess I'm kind of a kid too.

The early August mornin sun was warm on our faces. We were just creepin up the river, kinda slow like. By the looks of my crew, I figured it'd be best to slide into the day that way. Ol' Crockett was the worst lookin of the bunch with a face that looked like he had been peppered with birdshot. I could tell he was bein real careful with his poor ol' index finger, cause his milk had nearly drowned a few times. Ol' Boone had a chocolate milk mustache, river mud for war paint and that briar-eatin grin he always has. Me, well, I didn't have a mirror, so I'm sure I fit in just right with the whole bunch. One of the things I did notice was that I didn't have to tell either one of 'em to put on their life jackets. After the full night of adventure under our belt, we all had 'em hooked in place. At times in my life, I take inventory of what I am doin and where I am and I have to remember to breathe. I'm so thankful to God that this is my life. Even though it is hard at times, these are the moments that can become high points in our memories. Well, enough of all that ponderin, I hope we can all think about our blessings and realize that it could be very different.

That mornin was slow. We had caught 7 cats out of 18 hooks. We were along the left side of the Choctawhatchee River, near the mouth of Holmes Creek, which runs into the east side of the river. We found our cut into a slough that runs through Boynton Island and goes to The Dead River when the river is high. When maneuverin through the slough, if you don't watch for the faintly marked trees, you could find yourself wonderin through the backwater a while. Our goal was to stay on course to a half-acre spring pond not far from the main river, which is just the right size for three bush hooks. Last night, it produced for us again. Out of the two runs on the lines, we caught 3 catfish with 1 cut off right behind the head. This is fairly common. 4 others already shared the same fate; they were "yummy-in-the-tummy" for a hungry snappin turtle or perhaps, a gator. Seems normal to think that if dinner ain't puttin up a fight, you'd eat it too, right? As we make our way into the pond, my eyes are scannin the over hangin tree limbs for snakes and wasps nests. Under the bow of the boat I have an ol' banged up 20-gauge scatimous shot gun, just in case. I'll tell ya why I like a shotgun, cause your aim don't have to be as good if you find yourself in a "predicament." (Which is fancy for "in a mess.") I wonder if it would work on a wasp nest? Maybe the next time I see one; I'll have my revenge and bring 'em a little 20-gauge take out.

As we turn up through the cut and work our way through the swamps and trees in the slough, the mornin breeze brings in the smell of a campfire somewhere on the island. Is that bacon and eggs I smell? With the river up and all, I force myself to stay focused on the marks made on the trees by ol' timers to keep from losin our way to the pond. Clear water from the spring pond is not like the murky, muddy river water. When the clear spring water runs out of the pond, the river water mixes in with it and takes over the clear color. This is just the way it is for all the other creeks and streams that run into and become part of the mighty Choctawhatchee.

Once we reached the first bush hook, I could see through the clear water that we had a nice catfish. As I pulled it out though, there was nothin but a big, lifeless head left on the hook. The second bush hook was completely gone with just the line blowin in the breeze six inches above the water surface. The last bush hook was tied off to a willow limb hangin across the deepest corner of the spring fed pond and even from 20 yards away, it was plain to see the line zingin back and forth in the water. My crew, Boone and Crockett, readied themselves on the bow of the boat. It was Tommy's turn to check the line and Jonathan reluctantly held onto the tree limb, cause he doesn't really like the fairness of takin turns. Crockett gave the line the normal tug to flip the catfish in the boat, just as the big catfish comes to the top of the water, what a head; it's as big as a bait bucket! The catfish decides he's not gonna give up so easily and down he goes with the water splashin from the power of his big ol' tail. Crockett is pulled down to his knees in the bow of the boat yellin, "Daddy, I need some help!" I jumped to the bow with the boys and grabbed the line. I realized just how big a cat this one was as the line burned through my hands, breakin the willow limb it's tied to. With the limb in one hand and the line in the other, Crockett and myself hoist the huge blue catfish to the surface. All the splashin, sloshin, and hollerin echoin through the river swamp, no doubt drew the attention of everyone and anything close by. Finally, just as we pull the massive fish over the side of the boat, I saw it comin up fast from straight below. At first I didn't know what it was, that is, until his hugantic head came out of the water. It was obvious he was not a member of the welcomin committee once he hit the side of the boat with his mouth wide open. He was apparently drawn in by the commotion and the crack of his jaws slammin shut sounded like a high-powered rifle goin off. That crack started the beginnin of a nightmare, that even now brings an anxious sweat to my brow. This was his territory and we were a trespassin. A huge gator had staked his claim on this catfish! Unfortunately the gator was headed the same direction as the fish, which happened to be in the bottom of our boat. The lunge of the gator, as his body hugged the side of the boat, nearly caused the whole thing to flip over.

The tilt jolted me forward and the catfish was all that cushioned my fall, which was unpleasant e'nuff. Boone fell in the opposite direction and just before bellowin overboard, he managed to grab onto a willow tree branch. Crockett, on the other hand, didn't fare as well. The only good thing for him was that his fall was softened by the water. Crockett frantically tried to swim back to the boat as I was gettin up to help my boys. As the dread settled even deeper in my throat, I realized the gator made a new claim . . . on Crockett. He was positioned 'tween the boat and Tommy. Now Boone wouldn't like me tellin ya this, but he is a little feller and was havin a hard time holdin on. He managed to keep himself up a bit longer by kickin and splashin his feet, which was the distraction that saved Crockett's life. Boone will never let Crockett forget about him bein his hero. I only reacted like my daddy or any lovin daddy would and grabbed the long bow rope with the loop around my left hand. I guess I absent-mindedly did this to keep from losing the boat. With my right hand, I pulled my prized straight-bladed Cabelas skinnin knife out of the sheathe on my side and just as I dove off of the boat in midair, I hollered to the boys to get back in the boat. I landed smack dab on the gator's back right off the bat and I wrapped my legs around him like a bull rider. My left arm had a death grip around this dinosaur's back. I remembered the feelin of the boney ridges and humps in his armor. Maybe I saw too many of those old Tarzan movies as a boy. Now was not the time for me to play out my childhood fantasies. With the life of my boys at stake, though, I started doin the only thing I knew to do. With my right hand, I took my knife and as fast and as hard as I could, I worked on him, cuttin into his side under his right front leg and deep into his chest. For a brief moment, I felt like part of the Swamp People family and I've always wanted to say "choot em" real bad, but was quickly brought back to reality by the power of this gator's muscles as they tensed up from the terror of my blade deep into his chest. It was then he started the death roll, which was his attempt to get me off. With ev'ry roll, I felt the bow line constrictin, wrappin 'round us both, makin me a gator hood ornament. I think he knew he wasn't gonna get me off em after about the fifth or sixth wrap, but I was startin to run out of air. I had my right arm in his chest up to my elbow and then in a panic, I sliced and gashed even harder. The bow line was so tight around us that he couldn't roll anymore and I couldn't breathe. It felt like it was over for me. Many thoughts were quickly goin through my mind. "Oh God!" I prayed, "Is this how it's gonna end?" His muscles were beginnin to relax and I had a thousand questions . . . Have I killed him? Has he killed me? Are my boys alright? Did I pack extra underwear? Then I heard a beautiful sound from under the bow of the boat . . . an explosion! POW! A sound that could only come from that ol' rusted snake charmin 20-gauge. Then another explosion! He coulda done without the second shot, but ol' Crockett listens to his daddy, at least on the important things. "When in doubt, shoot anothern out," that's what I always say. I could hear my two little men that I call Boone and Crockett, hollerin, "Pull the rope, the gator has daddy pinned under em." God gave them the extra strength to face their fears, climb back into the boat, shoot the gator, and then flip him over. I suddenly felt myself coughin and chokin up the water that was quickly takin over my lungs. Boone kept hollerin to Crockett, "We have to help him; we just have to help him, his arm's gone." Openin my eyes to see that much blood on me was terrifyin. The water was stained with more blood as I pulled my arm out of the gator's chest. To a 7-year-old imagination, I can see how it appeared that my arm was missin. Other than a little "water weight," I was not injured. My boys, Boone and Crockett, had worked together to save my life. After gettin untangled from the bow rope and the huge alligator, I couldn't help but cry as I hugged my 2 boys, who now looked like men to me. At the edge of the spring pond, we nearly sunk the boat tryin to roll this giant gator into it. As we idled out of the slough and into the river, the 15'3" long gator's head lay just off the front of the bow and his tail was draggin in the water off the stern of my 14' boat. The sight of him drew such attention that by the time we got to the landin, the mob demanded I tell the story. What could I do but give the people what they wanted? News traveled fast and landed on the ears of 2 game and fish officers who wanted me to tell "my version" of the story. Turns out that my version was nearly identical to the one they heard. These two officers sent us on our way, sayin that all we went through was permit enough, and without proof of this gator, no one would believe me.

When you have an experience of this caliber, you can sort out your priorities and make the important stuff important again. That's just what I did; the next weekend, we had a big ol' fashion get-together. Our family and friends had plenty of fish to eat and for our fast food fans, we had gator mcnuggets. Look out Mickey-D, Yum-yum!

I really want to send a big "thanks" to Mike Mount for given me that fine skinnin knife. You're a sorta hero now, cause that knife saved our lives. What an adventure!

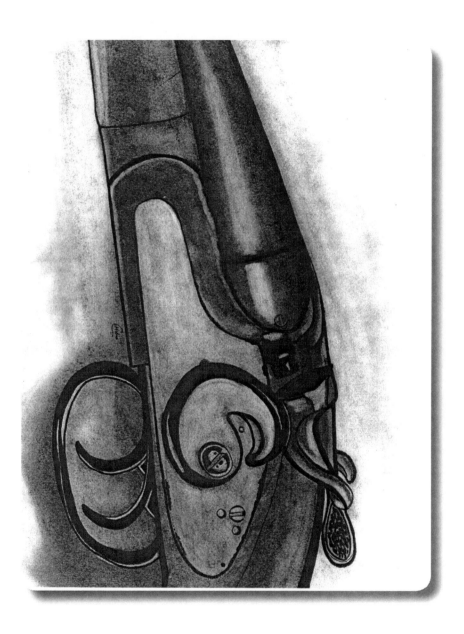

Grandpas Shotgun

There are many family heirlooms given to us when parents or grandparents pass on; some are not worth nothin, but they mean a lot to us. One of my most treasured heirlooms was my Grandpa Lipham's ol' double barrel muzzle loadin shotgun. I remember the day I first saw the gun, I thought my grandpa was Daniel Boone. He was my hero when I was a young boy. With his laugh and gift of story tellin, I'll never be able to forget him.

Most people don't use old antique guns like grandpas, but I couldn't wait. I was gonna be one of many generations in my family to hunt with the old gun. Every time I hold it, I have dreams about the crack in the stock and I wonder about the story behind each and ev'ry nick & scratch.

I only got to hunt with the gun one time, but that day will go down as a huntin trip that will make family history. I know I don't look like it, but my family has a lot of Creek Indian in our bloodline. My brother Michael and I were taught at a very young age, the art of "stalking". Now I don't mean the kind you get put in jail for like ol' Cousin Larry. I mean the kind were you slip through the woods and only move about 30 yards in an hour; it's sorta like yer invisible. My dad, Tommy, taught us how to avoid steppin on sticks or crunchin leaves. As we got older, we moved slowly and thought cautiously like any wild animal would, because with them it is a matter of life or death. So, that's how you have to look at stalkin. I've moved through the woods impatiently before even knowin there was somethin there, only to spook it off because the animal waited me out, not the other way around. Stalkin is a lost art of the true hunter. Stalkin and bein "naturally" scent-free is what has made my huntin career so productive.

Muzzle loadin season here in Northwest Florida always falls the weekend before Thanksgiving. The excitement of gettin to go huntin has brought me many a sleepless nights. I believe there are a lot of people who love huntin so much, that they'd go even if they had to hunt with a spear. I made plans this time to go over to the Choctawhatchee River with my friend Kyle. Kyle had carried me over to that wild river several years before. What a great feelin to get away and camp on the side of the Choctawhatchee. Just leave me there with the crackle of a campfire and the sound of the water flowin through the snags and the stumps of that mighty river, but come back in about a week cause I'll probably need more food by then.

We had arrived a day early on Thursday mornin, set up camp, took a deep breath and admired the surroundins. We decided to go squirrel huntin while we were scoutin for deer and hogs; I believe in killin two birds with one rock. I was in one boat and Kyle was in another with his son, Conner. I know for a fact that that boy is not gonna miss any fishin or huntin trip, if'n he can help it. We found plenty of sign and got our game plan together on where we would each hunt the next mornin. I remembered that I had found several years before, as I was goin around The Dead River side of Boynton

Island, a taller stand of hardwoods that were twice the height of all the rest of the swamp. I was reminded of this as I was maneuverin my boat in and met up with Mr. Gator Brown, an old friend of Kyle's. I asked em bout that ridge and he told me that what I had seen was a 300-acre ridge of mostly huge White Oaks that were surrounded by a large swamp. The swamp had mud, waist deep in most places around the ridge, so it's completely locked with no way in by foot travel. Mr. Brown said he knew of one moonshiner that ran his business on that ridge over fifty years ago. The rumor was that he would go up to the island with a small boat, like a pirogue. The ol' moonshiner would go up the creek that flowed not far from Blue Pitcher Bend, where the creek would branch out to the huge flowin spring that comes out from under a massive Magnolia tree in the west corner of the ridge.

In scoutin the area again, I wanted to try my best to get on that ridge. I just couldn't get if off my mind. The river was real high cause of all the rain the week before from Tropical Storm Chrissy. I knew this was my best chance to get up there. It was now or never! I spent most of the day markin my way through the Cypresses with red ribbon, slippin my way into the backwater to get to "moonshine ridge," proudly named that by me. Like Hansel, I had clearly marked a trail so I could find my way back. Now I know why no one had hunted this place, the trees in this swamp were so close together that I could barely get my 14' Scandy White between many of the Cypresses. At 2:00 in the afternoon, seein land couldn't have been sweeter, even if I was a Pilgrim on the Mayflower. I was finally here, lookin at a stand of some of the tallest hardwoods I had ever seen, huge White Oak ac'rns floated all around the boat. It was sorta romantic; I was fallen in love with the beauty of the woods all over again. Now, don't be jealous honey, you're still the one for me.

That night, after supper, we discussed what we'd found while scoutin that day and we each laid out our strategies for the next day's hunt. I could hardly sleep while waitin for mornin to come and for my first chance to use the most admired gun I ever set my eyes on. I felt that I had ev'rythang right to hunt the virgin ground of Moonshine Ridge. What I wouldn't give for Grandpa to have been able to share this excitement with me. I laid in my tent listenin to the snap, crackle, pop of the fire and the flow of the river until it lulled me to sleep.

The next mornin we got up well before daylight and packed our grub for the hunt. Kyle could tell from the night before that I was on a mission; he could see it in my eyes. It was about 60 degrees when we got up and unfortunately in Florida, that's normal. A bit warm fer me, but ain't no use in complainin. The huntin is usually mighty good, cause I reckon the animals get used to the weather. I sorta get the heebie jeebies when I'm runnin the Choctawhatchee River in the dark. It's not if yer gonna hit a stump, it's when, and hopefully yer prepared for the sudden stop. That 40-horse Honda ain't never let me down and today was no exception. I had to use a pole the last 100 yards through the tightest trees, but I finally had my feet on Moonshine Ridge.

It was just gettin red in the East, so I moved in about 50 yards from the boat and sat down against a huge hickory. Bein early in the year, a lot of the leaves were still on the trees. I nearly fell asleep from the slight sound the wind makes when it blows through a tall stand of trees. Just about makes a tree hugger out of ya, cause it's rare for them to get that tall anymore. I suppose there is too much money to be made in trees and not enough patience to wait for them to grow. The trees here on Moonshine ridge had never been cut.

Once the sun had come up, good stalkin was all I had in mind. I was truly in awe of this ridge; deer and hog tracks covered the ground. As the mornin light was clear, the ridge was alive with squirrels and birds. Another great method of stalkin is takin shape of whatever is around you. I was comin up very slowly on a palmetto flat and I knew I could take the shape. I call this move by its name, the palmetto. It may look ridiculous to some, but bein fully camouflaged and blendin in is the key. While doin the palmetto before, I actually stalked up and touched a doe.

Movin on in through the palmettos, stalkin up to the creek that flows through the ridge, somethin caught my eye. I was slowly scannin in ev'ry direction and at first I thought it was a burnt stump stickin up through the thick brush. Upon closer inspection, whatever it was loomed larger and larger. There was no mistaken it now, I could make out the form of what it was . . . about a 500 pound black bear was bedded up right in the middle. The sight of the bear made my knees quiver like a Chiquita in a Cuisinart. This redneck Garden of Eden has a devil too.

My stalkin abilities were then put to the test. All thoughts of huntin were out of my mind and my attention was put to gettin past this coal black bruiser. I was not prepared for another encounter with a big bear like before . . . well, that's another story.

It took me about an hour to stalk from within 20 yards of the bear to nearly 50 yards, a feat in itself, especially goin through palmettos without any noise. I had made my way up against a small creek. I was still in some danger, but with him a sleepin, I thought I was in the clear. Think again! All of a sudden at my feet, I heard the familiar sound that no woodsman wants to hear. It was a slight rattle at first, and then it began to zing its rattles. Layin at my feet was the biggest rattlesnake I ever did see. He was all coiled up and looked like a bullfrog sittin on a spare tire.

I was frozen in my tracks and just fixin to maneuver myself to take his head off with the double barrel, when a poppin sound came from across the creek. My, my, my! Just across the creek, under one of the giant White Oaks was the buck of a lifetime. He was a massive 12-point that looked like he had baby oak trees on his head! This giant buck was eatin ac'rns less than 30 yards from me. Right behind him, I could see the remains of the 50-year old moonshine still and a small cabin. My mind was a racin, what was I gonna do now? Takin a deep breath and lookin slowly to my left, I saw two big hogs. They were anywhere from three to four hundred pounds apiece and at the edge of the creek. Their tusks were so big that as they walked across the ridge, they were clearin the brush on either side. Scannin now to the right, just a short piece away from me, was a covey of over 100 quail, big as chickens, drinkin their fill from the creek. This place was alive with more game then I ever could of imagined.

Maintainin my palmetto stance, fully camouflaged and scent free, I was undetected from ev'rythang, but this huge rattler. I had made up in my mind that 'tween the big bear and the huge rattlesnake, I probably would not make it out of these woods alive. I decided to go ahead and take my best shot at a once in a lifetime buck. I slowly raised the heavy double barrel muzzle-loadin shotgun, bein careful not to spook the monster buck. With heart poundin and hands tremblin, I aimed straight for the buck and squeezed off both barrels at the same time, not realizin that I had left the ramrod in one of the barrels. BOOM!! The ramrod shot out of the gun like an arrow, all the way through the hugantic 12-point buck and dropped em like a sack of taters. The ramrod caused both barrels to explode. The left barrel went to the left hand side of the creek and killed both of the big hogs. The right barrel went down the right hand side of the creek and killed the covey of quail, all hunderd of em. The gun had kicked so hard that the stock broke off, bounced off my shoulder, flipped backards and hit the coal black bear right-square 'tween his eyes, killin em graveyard dead. The explosion caused the firin pin to get cherry-red hot and drop on the head of the rattlesnake, endin his life.

Go figure, Kyle and Conner didn't believe me. All they heard was one loud shot bellow and echo through the river swamp like a cannon. That is, until they had to help me haul out three boat loads full of game.

Wow, I knew that this gun was special, but I never knew how special until that moment. What a bittersweet end to this treasured heirloom. What's left of my Grandpa's double barrel muzzle loadin shotgun now hangs on my wall, right next to my prized 12-point mount, so I can admire it from my bearskin rug, while wearin my snakeskin boots. I will always cherish that gun and it will go down in my family's history.

Grant & Lee

I have been blessed over the years to hunt in some beautiful places. The woods I long for most, though, are the woods around my Grandpa's farm. The farm is run down now. Broken fences, weeds and fallen trees are what litter the ground and the farmhouse has fallen in around itself. The old barn, well, she is mostly piled up on the ground, but memories are not made of wood and they hold up real good.

My family was fortunate enough to acquire 120 acres of the homestead property up on Econfina Creek. Those 120 acres are some of the purdiest woods I have ever tromped through and some of my most excitin memories happened there. I do believe I have had more adventures on that one parcel of land than any other.

Over the last few years, we have been groomin those woods; we have chopped a few trees, cleared a few spots, put out corn and fed more deer than we ever killed. With the amount of corn them rascals was eatin, we knew the deer were thick and the huntin was gonna be good. Now, all that hard work is payin off since my kids are gettin old enough to go huntin with me, my daddy and other family and friends.

As the 2009/2010 huntin season was drawin near, the outlook was very hopeful. We had pictures on our trail cams of some very nice bucks. However, the huntin spots up here around Fountain, Florida, are no different than most other huntin areas; we have our fair share of poachers too. We did manage to get some of them on the trail cameras, but the smart ones took the camera when they left.

In early November, I found evidence of what would prove to make this huntin season a life-changin year. It was a six-point buck with a hole right through em. The hole looked as if a poacher had shot the deer and it had somehow gotten away. Then, Thanksgiving weekend, I found a nice little four-point and a spike, both with the same fatal injuries. Both animals had what appeared to be bullet holes and the four-point looked like he had been shot more than once. The entrance and exit wounds looked to be the same size and this was very puzzlin to me. There weren't many bucks comin through the food plots like they were just a month ago. Now, these two bucks were killed and left where they fell. What did it all mean?

I put in a call to the Game and Fish Commission and kinda went over what had been goin on. They said they would step up a patrol in the area. I also called a good friend, Larry Grainger, who happens to be a deputy sheriff and assigned to the Fountain district. He said he would be happy to investigate and keep an eye out as well.

Things seemed to be lookin up! The officers' presence and the extra activity in the area seemed to have taken care of the poachin problem. At least we didn't find any evidence of trespassin on the property.

January 10, 2010, it changed again. Daddy and my son, Tommy "Crockett" Kelley, found a huge eight-point dead right beside a big ol' scrape. There was blood everywhere, the ground was all torn up, and just as before, this big fella looked to be shot. There were two holes through his chest and two more through his neck. The strangest thing was that the left side of his horns, with a four-inch base, was broke off about half way up and layin twenty yards away.

All four of the deer were found in about a thirty-acre parcel of the property and were less than three hundred yards off the graded road. My wife was gettin kinda concerned and didn't want me or Daddy takin the boys out to hunt until the poachin issue was resolved.

I was sick. All the hard work we had put into plantin, placin our stands at just the right spot and puttin out corn was for naught. I felt I had no control over what was goin on at our place. The law enforcement officers from the Game and Fish, and the deputies from the sheriff's office were as baffled as I was. Why, the Game and Fish fellas had even brought up the robotic deer to see what they could catch. They did get a couple of poachers, but that was before the eight-point was killed. I reckon one of the hardest parts about the whole situation, was why someone would go to the trouble to poach those bucks, what I thought were some very fine bucks, and then just leave 'em. I sure-nuff would've had that eight-point mounted without raisin an eyebrow and threw the other ones on the grill.

I talked with my good friend and our office manager, Marty Schrier. We figgered it was time to take matters into our own hands. Now Marty, good man that he is, is from New Jersey. I am a southern boy, born and raised here in Florida. Marty is not a huntin kind of feller and I have been huntin since I could walk good. Marty is real book smart though. As for me, well, let's just say I'm magazine smart. Anyways, Marty pulled up some aerial pictures of our land and we studied the roads, trails, nooks and crannies and tried to figure out the most likely way the buck killer could be comin in and still go undetected. We finally came to the conclusion that he was usin an old two-rut loggin road over by the farmhouse. This road comes onto the property, passes by the farmhouse and goes on around by what's left of the barn. The timber on the place is forty-year-old pines, the poacher could come down that loggin road, hole up on the farm place and move through the tall trees, and no one would be none the wiser. We put our heads together and came up with a plan.

Marty was gonna come up and stay with me in the cabin for about a week or so, takin turns listenin for any night huntin activity. Now keep in mind, the cabin is about four hundred yards from the homestead, so we could easily hear a shot ringin through the big timber. By day, we would be set up in the camouflaged pop-up blind. We had the ice chest filled up with RC Colas, sandwiches and snacks. We had us a couple of good chairs, those kind with the feet rests; we were on a mission and in for the long haul. My ol' Yankee friend was puttin his Air Force Special Ops trainin together with my Navy Seal trainin and we were determined to put an end to the reign of terror over my family, Grandpa's ol' farm and the deer herd.

The first two days were quiet, both day and night. Then, on the third mornin, as we were headin in to set up the tent before daylight, we came across about a 160 pound, nine-point buck, dead in the road. Like the others, he had a hole right through his neck. This big deer was in full rut. (Full rut means that he was lookin for a girlfriend) We decided to leave him there and put the blind on the loggin road to see if anyone came back for him. For the mission's sake, we hoped they would try.

We had pictures of these bucks on our trail cams early in the season, but now that the rut was comin in, only doe were showin up. We were hopin the poachers might get a little excited and a lot careless, what with the bucks on the move and all.

This kind of huntin was startin to rattle my nerves a little. I mean, when we catch the ones responsible for this slaughterin, what will happen? My biggest worry was a heated confrontation, so me and Marty both were well armed. Marty had my Ruger mini 14 and I had my ol' trusty Mossberg 3 1/2 magnum.

It was very cold that January mornin and my feet were frozen. I thought the sun would never come up and chase the chill away. About eight o'clock, things began to happen. Sittin in our chairs in the camo blind, with just one window open, we were cold and mentally exhausted. We were positioned on the loggin road about 50 yards from the graded road and about forty yards from the ol' toppled barn. I saw a flash comin through the woods from the graded roadside. It was a big doe with a big ten-point buck chasin her. I told Marty to shoot em, cause he's a real good buck and at least the buck-killers wouldn't get em. We decided to wait it out and see what turned up. When she got to Grandpa's barn, she stopped and was actin real nervous like. For a long time she was struttin around and flickin her ears back and forth. The ten-point buck was doin the same thang! What was spookin these deer, we wondered.

Marty had his gun up, ready to end this buck's life, but before he could pull the trigger, less than forty yards from us, right behind the barn and outta nowhere, we saw a streak of lightnin. Now I'm not talkin about the weather kind, I'm talkin about the super-hero kind. That big ten-point was nailed by the lightnin and knocked to the ground right in front of us! I looked at Marty, and then at the lifeless buck, back at Marty again; I was awed and amazed! I whispered, "Can you believe this?" My next thought was to shoot this creature, but before I could get the words out of my mouth, Marty's shot rang out. The ol' Yankee had shot this mutant right in the neck and his head went down, yet he was still runnin right for us! It was as if the world were in slow motion. A two-headed monster and I mean MONSTER was still a comin. Marty had shot and broken one of his necks and I was unloadin the 3 1/2 inch magnum double-ought buckshot as fast as I could squeeze the trigger. As I was about to pump the fourth shot into the freakish thing, the camo tent caught me under the arms and sent me flyin backards. Ol' Marty had took off runnin the other DI-rection and just took the tent right on with em. We both got all tangled up and toppled to the ground, like we was playin a game of Twister or somethin. That huge two-headed beast crashed smack-dab into our chairs as he finally fell to the ground. When the dust settled and we got untangled, we were shocked to find a twenty-one point, two headed buck with only three feet tween him and us. Can you say r-e-l-i-e-f?

This was a massive deer! He weighed 242 pounds and had a foot like a calf. A two-headed buck; why I never heard of such. In his rack around the bases, instead of bark from scrapin and rubbin trees, there was blood and hair and more stuck to the tines. As we continued to examine the buck, the answers to the mysterious deaths of the other five deer were becomin apparent. The other bucks that came into his territory never stood a chance.

Each head had a normal rack on the outside with thirteen and fourteen inch tines. There was also a drop tine on each one. Then, on the inner side of the racks, toward each other, the horns were non-typical; they were long, kinda like a cow horn that kept on growin. They were fifteen to sixteen inches long and went straight up with kickers goin off the bases. This was the part of the buck's horns, on each head mind you, that was puttin the holes through the other bucks' necks. His two heads were double-teamin one. This monster two-headed buck would do the same damage anywhere, givin his hugantic size.

Marty, the non-hunter-Yankee-smart guy had just got in on the kill of a lifetime. This was most certainly a one-of-a-kind trophy buck. We were torn on whether or not to call the Game and Fish Commission to share the trophy buck and we finally decided against it for many reasons. The biggest bein all the attention and traffic it would bring up here to our piece of paradise on Grandpa's farm.

This is the first we have released about this 242-pound, twenty-one point, two-headed monster buck that we have named the "Grant & Lee". Grant for my Yankee friend Marty and Lee, for my great southern heritage. The "Grant & Lee" is only fittin for such a warrior of the wild.

Now, with the big boy dead, the terror of Grandpa's farm was finally over. With an unofficial score of 253 7/8, unofficial because of his two heads, he is still a world record in his own right. I did have his jawbone aged at six and a half to seven and a half years old; due to the sandy soil around this part of northwest Florida, that was as close as we could get. We have done an extensive investigation and after lots of trackin and research, we have found that this buck lived on the nineteen-acre stand of tall pine timber, not even one-hundred yards from a well-traveled, graded road.

Goin back over all the cameras that we had placed around, we think we may have one picture of him on the trail cam. Course, he looked like two bucks back in the shadows and as soon as the camera flashed, that's all she wrote. He only needed one time to learn a lesson and he never got close to another camera. Too bad for him, there is ne'er a second chance when crossin the path of a Yank and a Hillbilly!

The "Grant & Lee" buck thrived on Grandpa's farm. He or maybe it's they, had a sleepin place wallered out where he would lay up against the ol' collapsed barn. We found three years of horn sheds within fifty yards of the barn. The soon to be world-renowned "Grant & Lee" buck lived and died at my Grandpa's farm.

Has grandpa taken you behind the barn lately?

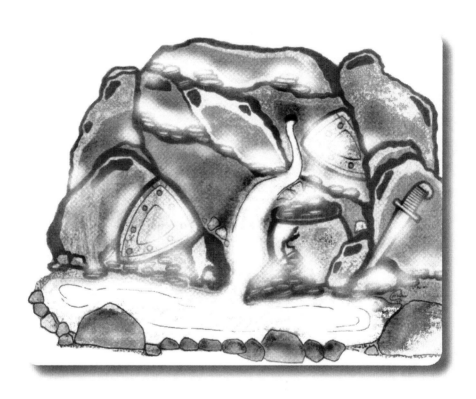

The Fountain

B ein born and raised in Northwest Florida, what some folks call
L.A., for Lower Alabama, has brought me more adventure and
excitement than I ever could have imagined. And if you're not from
around here, there is one thing you need to understand, the natives
don't live on the beach. We natives are true Southerners. We fish,
hunt and crawl through the woods, rivers and creeks found in this
area. We have all kinds of terrain: stuff like oak ridges, palmetto flats,
cypress swamps and pine forests. Around these places, you're likely
to find rattlesnakes, cottonmouths, bears, gators and on occasion, a
panther.

Most of the rural people, like my family, farm to make that little
extra to put on the table and to help make ends meet. My Grandpa
Lipham had a farm. I remember how I just loved gettin to go up to
see Grandpa. It would give me the grins just thinkin about stayin up
there at that farm for the whole weekend. In the summertime, Grandpa
would put you to work though, you'd be pickin peas or hoein the
garden or helpin Grandmother put up preserves. Nevertheless, even
with all that work, there was adventure around ev'ry corner.

Along with all those crops and vegetables came varmints. One of the worst was coons, especially on the corn crops, so Grandpa always kept a few coon dogs. I just loved his ol' coonhounds. We really got after those coons, too. Many a night we would tree as many as four or five. Even today, on a still night, around a good campfire, I imagine I can hear the hounds echoin through the Econfina Creek bottoms. As Grandpa got older and he couldn't ramble through the woods at night anymore, I started goin with my Uncle Eddie Lipham. I guess we just got coon crazy cause we'd be going three and four nights a week.

Durin my high school years, that coon huntin spread like a virus. Folks from ev'ry walk and social status would go off on a Friday night coon huntin with us. I thought coon huntin would be a part of my life forever. Then, Hurricane Opal hit in 1995. That was the beginnin of a chain of events that would change this freckle faced young man forever.

When a hurricane's a comin, and we know it's gonna be a bad one, many times we open the dog pens and let our hounds run free. Why, you ask? You've heard that ol' sayin about havin enough sense to get in out of the rain, right? Well, dogs and most other animals know it very well. They'll be safer out of the pens, cause God gave them a natural instinct to read and sense the weather and act accordingly.

As we were monitorin the weather, it became apparent that Hurricane Opal was gonna hit a little to the west of us. We know that the east side of a storm is the most dangerous side due to the counter clockwise spin. This storm was gettin pretty bad pretty quick, so we boarded up our windows and battened down the hatches. I put my new trackin collar on ol' Huck and turned loose one of the finest Treein Walker coonhounds in these parts. I knew there'd be no tellin where he would be after the storm, but findin Huck would be easier thanks to the trackin collar.

We have been blessed over the years not to get much hurricane damage, even though there have been several storms hit our area. We Natives know they are dangerous and not to be taken lightly. That's why the Native Floridians live inland, not on the beach.

Once we got the house all safe and secure, we headed over to my daddy's house, where my family and myself always weather out these kinds of storms. For those of you who know my daddy, Tommy Riley, you know there's none better at the helm of a BBQ grill!

When the power goes out durin the storm, we get all excited. That means its grillin time and what a feast we have! Food and fellowship with other family members and friends from our church becomes more like a treat than a retreat. We just plain out enjoy ourselves.

Opal was a fast movin storm and passed by in a hurry. After she moved on, I left my family at my daddy's house and went to assess the damage. There were many downed trees and no power, but other than that, ev'rythang was fine. Now my attention went to findin Huck. I knew I needed to hunt Huck down, now that it was safe enough to get out. If not, the creeks would continue to rise and ol' Huck, a five year old, gritty, hard treein, half-eared, scarred up coon dog, would be huntin a coon just as soon as he crawled from wherever he had taken shelter. Ol' Huck was as coon crazy as I was.

I had been taught not to get attached to huntin dogs like you would a pet. I have to say, most of the time I had no problem with that and hunted my hounds in the way they were bred to perform. I knew there was always a possibility that the dog may not come back. They were liable to get snake bit, run over by a car, or just plain out stolen. Huck was different. More than any other huntin dog, he was a companion. He obeyed commands and would even ride in the back of the truck. This is very uncharacteristic of most coonhounds, even most huntin dogs in general. At times, due to their breedin, they can be high-strung and folks need a dog box in the back of the truck to keep the hounds under control.

Certain things about Huck started goin through my mind. On the soft side, he loved my young'uns and what he wouldn't do for a tater chip!! Why, he'd sit, roll over and beg and beg for that tater chip, Doritos was his favorite. On the tough side, there weren't no better, fast movin, loud strikin, bark chewin coonhound in these parts. Ev'rybody who has ever hunted with him has always been impressed with his easy handlin and his "go yonder" huntin ability.

I commenced hollerin for him around the house with no answer. Good for me he had that trackin collar on and I had the trackin machine. I rode around the neighborhood and helped some friends and neighbors move trees and debris out of the roads and off their roofs, just bein neighborly, but all the while givin out a yell every now and then for Huck. There was no sign of him on that first day, but I wasn't worried, yet. I figured I'd find him laid up on the porch at first light. I went on to the house and fired up the generator, if'n I didn't, the smell from the freezer would put me in the doghouse with Huck, once he returned.

The next mornin, I got up and looked around the house and there was still no sign of Huck. I decided to make a pass around with my trackin machine to see what I could find. My effort was in vain. Maybe I should search a wider area, I thought. I took the main highways and roads around five square miles of my house. I finally got a faint signal on the trackin machine not far from Econfina Creek, just south of Highway 20. This area was familiar to me as I had coon hunted it over the years in L.B. and Floyd Nelson's Bear

Head Huntin Lease. Willard Kelly and I have treed a pile of coons in this area with no problem. Well, with the exception of Casper, the very unfriendly coon.

Casper was a solid white albino coon with eyes that would light up the night sky when you shined him. I'll never forget the first time we treed this coon, it was a cold and still November night. We treed him in a short pine and at first glance, we thought he was a possum. As we got closer to that short tree, we could see the coon markins on his face and tail. His mask and the rings on his tail were a brownish-red color. One other thing that stuck out to me was that Casper only had two toes on his right foot, which explained why such a big coon climbed such a small tree. Although, he was as big as he was, he couldn't climb very well with that crippled foot.

While we were still checkin Casper out, he bailed out of the tree right square on top of ol' Huck. He was only a couple of years old and Casper the unfriendly coon made quick work of chewin up one of Huck's ears and scarrin up his face. Huck ended up rippin off about a third of Casper's tail. As they rolled into a cat-claw briar thicket with plenty of squalls and yelps, Casper broke free and led Huck on a three-hour tour with Huck buglin out a bark ev'ry breath of the way.

The chase wound through Cat Creek right on up to a tree just south of the Patronis' property fence line, off Enfinger Road. It was a huge, hollow, 500 year old live oak tree that spanned about 100 yards in each direction. Willard and I would make many a trip behind Huck and his coon dog, Suzee, to this hollow den tree. It was the only tree that Casper would tree in. That is if he didn't trick the hounds before he got to his den, throwin them off his track by markin another tree but never goin up in it. The coon and the hounds were schoolin each other.

Willard and I hunted Casper for three years. After many long chases through the creeks and branches in pursuit of him, we decided he was too much fun to shoot. The chase and tree was better than the kill. Casper is no doubt, the reason Huck and Suzee became two of the best coonhounds in the southeast.

While I was drivin over the flooded Econfina Creek Bridge on Highway 20, I called Willard on the CB radio. I told him I figgered Huck was at Casper's den tree. As I was talking to Willard, one of my other good huntin buddies, Terry Segers, broke in, said he was at his aunt's house on the creek and could clearly hear Huck across the bottom.

Terry has hunted deer, coon, you name it, with me for years. Terry was a good hunter and was always ready. I was glad to have someone like him with me, as we didn't know what kind of obstacles we might encounter. Lookin back now, I was sure glad Terry was always ready for an adventure, cause we was fixin to have one!

We drove around, under and even over trees, through deep waters and washouts. Four-wheel drives are well worth their money to a hunter, especially to this hunter tryin to get back in the woods where Huck was treed. As it was gettin dark, Terry and I were within walkin distance of where ol' Huck was barkin up a storm. Well, barkin down a storm. Huck had Casper treed at his den tree all right, but the tree was blown over. The beautiful 500-year-old tree had toppled over from the storm. The giant had fallen, takin down a huge stand of other trees with it. It was sad to see such a majestic tree layin on the ground, a tree that used to take my breath away when I looked up at it.

Huck was at the base of the tree, with roots stretchin up in the air some 25 feet. Hurricane Opal and her destruction had changed ev'rythang. Terry got to Huck first and was barkin treed. A good hunter can tell when the dog's bark has changed from runnin the coon to treein the coon. This time, instead of treein up, Huck was treein down. He was lookin in the big hole where the root system of the gigantic oak used to be. As I got closer to him, Terry hollered to me, "You got to see this!"

Walkin to the edge of the hole, I could see an old war like shield partially coverin the openin to a cave. There are many of these caverns along Econfina Creek, so I am fairly familiar with them. But this one was just like what the Spanish would have used to hide their treasures in the New World. They would block off the cave with the shield and then plant a tree on the top of it. When they returned, the tree would have grown around the shield and left a hollow place at the base of the tree. Only the Spaniards would know which tree it was that was hidin their cavern full of treasure.

I heard that in 1985, a dolomite quarry company unearthed seven such blocked off entrances to one huge cave. It housed a pile of gold, silver and Indian beadwork with many different weapons.

When I got to ol' Huck, he had his head shoved up under the edge of the shield that was now only partially coverin the cavern's entrance. Gettin the shield free of the vines was a job, but Terry helped me pull and tug until it was out of the way. I took my flashlight and shined down into the cave, it was huge! Best I could tell it went way up under the Patronis property chain-link fence. I could hear water runnin through the massive cavern.

My first mistake was not tyin Huck back out of the way. He knew Casper was in there and the next thing I knew, he bailed off after that ol' coon. He landed about 10 feet down, through the clutter of vines and roots, face to face with Casper, the unfriendly coon. Huck hadn't forgot Casper; it was as if he remembered where the scars and notched up ear had come from three years earlier.

When Huck got to the bottom, the fight began, squallin and a yelpin. I couldn't stand not knowin. Without sayin a word, Terry knew what I was thinkin. When I was climbin down through the vines, he told me to be careful. I asked Terry to stay there, no matter what happened or what he heard; I was gonna need him to guide me out of the cave when the time came.

On my way down, there was a cool breeze comin up through the cavern with a sweet smell that I won't soon forget. Once I reached the floor, I could tell the room opened up. The fight was up around the curve so I took off t'ward them. My second mistake was not bringin my gun. Well, at least I had my waterproof flashlight; if I ran into somethin, I reckon I could blind em. As I got closer to where the action was, I could feel a mist on my face comin from somewhere up ahead. I must have covered a quarter-mile when I began to think that this place looked familiar. It reminded me of the Marianna Caverns State Park. It had those, what do you call 'em, you know, those limestone icicles stickin up and hangin down?

There was a stream flowin through the third big room that I came to. The stream was crystal clear and I stepped too close to the edge and slipped right into the water. Some stream, it was only two feet wide but ev'ry bit of six feet deep. I weren't prepared for a swim, but I did have sense enough to hold onto my sidekick, the flashlight, as I sunk all the way to the bottom. Once I climbed out, the fightin sounds of Huck and Casper were so loud that I just knew they would be around the next bend.

Finally, I caught up to Huck and Casper. All I could hear was squallin, yelpin, fightin, and water a churnin. Three streams, each one comin from a different tunnel, came into this room and dropped off about four feet into a pool. The fight was on a ridge 'tween two waterfalls. I kept noticin flashes of gold ev'ry few seconds as Huck and Casper tangled up in the fight of their lives. I climbed closer to the fight, the squeals and squalls were drownin out the waterfalls. Then, I saw it! There were gold pieces all around the room. Spanish breastplates, helmets and a bunch of swords were also in there. One sword had a gold handle with jewels on it, it looked expensive. I could not believe what was before my very eyes! As the two fought, gold coins were fallin off the edge of the bluff. Couldn't nothin be better than this for a man, a good fight in a room full of treasure!

When I shined my light on Huck and Casper, Casper broke free and lunged off the edge into the churnin pool below. Wouldn't ya know, Huck was right behind em and into the water they went. Watchin them with my flashlight, I noticed swirls in the water, it was a right powerful whirlpool they were in. All of a sudden, the animals disappeared. They were literally sucked down into the tornado water. I thought to myself, what a terrible end to two such fine adversaries.

I thought I was hearin things when I heard Huck barkin again, but he was behind the honeycomb limestone wall on the opposite side of the cave. I was thinkin to myself, how in the world am I gonna get around to the other side of that wall? Walkin t'ward the wall, I could tell Huck and Casper were on the move again, cause his barks were gettin harder to hear as they moved away from me.

Shinin my light around in every direction, lookin for a way to Huck, I saw Indian pots full of gold coins. Some pots were busted and the coins were spillin out all over the place. Looking up, there was another shield on the ceilin. Somewhere up there, above ground, there was another tree with a hollow at ground level; there could be even more entrances to this place.

I was now soakin wet, didn't know what to do, and had to get back out of here. I knew Terry was not gonna believe me, so I grabbed a handful of coins and stuck 'em in my pocket. I backtracked my way back through the cave, hollerin for Terry as I went. He finally heard me and led me the rest of the way out. I sure was glad he came along.

I told Terry about the cave and the stream and then the treasures. Course, he thought I was spinnin a yarn, since I have plenty of fruit of the looms. So, I reached in my pocket and showed him the handful of gold coins. Terry was a believer now and just as excited as I was.

While he was a waitin on me, Terry had gone back to the truck and got the trackin machine. I have to say; those boys at Quick Track have got a fine system. The signal was faint, but easy to follow. The big tree had fallen across the Patronis' fence, so we climbed over and followed the trackin machine. We went northwest a good ways and passed a few openins in the ground which were kinda like skylights into the caverns that I had just been in.

The signal was strong on the trackin machine now, but we couldn't hear a sound of ol' Huck or Casper. Terry could tell I was very concerned about my coon dog. We started up over a ridge and could hear the sound of runnin water not too far from Econfina.

As we got to the shallow water stream, flowin swiftly from a five-foot limestone cave, Terry, holdin the trackin machine, hollered out to me. "Huck has to be right here!" he said. He turned the machine down and the signal was sayin he was right here. All the pieces were startin to come together. Right in front of my eyes, on the edge of this wide stream was Huck's trackin collar. Beside the collar was a scar-faced, notch-eared, Treeing Walker coonhound pup. Not even 3 feet behind him was a solid white kitten coon missin three toes on his front foot and part of his tail.

I went to my knees and by this time, Terry was beside me. We were both speechless. These two had fought their way through the Fountain of Youth. They were still alive and crawlin around the water's edge. We picked 'em up and I wrapped 'em in my shirt to dry 'em off. Walkin back to our trucks, Terry and I asked questions that we knew would mostly go unanswered.

The next mornin, we went back to the entrance of the cavern, covered it with logs and took the shield with us. We went back one more time after that. The fence had been repaired and heavy equipment had cleaned the huge ol' tree off of the Patronis' fence. It took a lot to move the large fallen tree and debris out of the way and in the process, they had covered the entrance. This leads me to my third mistake . . . not wearin pants with more pockets, but I still have my five gold coins and Terry has his.

Huck and Casper, well, we raised them up again, and this time, instead of enemies, they grew up as the best of friends. They lived about ten years after the Fountain and are now buried, side by side, in my backyard.

We didn't tell anyone about the treasure, cause ain't nothin worse than watchin a redneck tryin to train his dogs to hunt gold, stead of coons. The feud between the Hatfield's and McCoy's would look like pigs fightin over fresh slop compared to my buddies fightin over a bunch of loot. Ev'ry single one of em is a member of the NRA. There'd be more bloodshed than if the Red Cross was given five dollers for donations durin a depression.

We were goin back once the mystery behind our new pup and kitten coon died down. We knew we would need a tractor to dig out the cave and were savin up and makin our plans. To our dismay, the Patronis' family built a business right up against their property line. They called it, "Econfina Spring Water." I'm afraid that the closest we'll ever get to the Fountain of Youth now is drinkin a bottle of that refreshin water. I have noticed a few less wrinkles lately and my skin does feel softer than a baby's butt.

The Original Exterminator

L et me tell you 'bout an ol' man by the name of "Romer." He's from Bear Creek, which is a little community in Northwest Florida. There are still a few family farms there today with some genuine southern country folk. At 123 years old, Romer still gets around better'n I do.

I remember the first time I laid eyes on this woodsman. I was up at my grandpa's farm, north of Fountain on Econfina Creek. It was the year 1970 and I was a mite 6 years old. In this area of the south, Romer was known for his many stories and adventures that tell the history of the wild; why I'd bet, if'n I was old nuff to, that he was friends with Davy Crockett! When I wasn't in school, hangin out with my grandpa was what I liked to do most, cause what little fella wouldn't want to hang out with his hero.

I remember the easy gait of the ol' horse comin up the rutted trail to the barn. On its back sat Romer, a man with a long gray beard. One of the first things I was intrigued by was that he somehow held onto the back of that horse with no hands. Now either it already knew the way to the barn or that ol' man steered with his knees.

I'm not for sure which it was, but it was miraculous. As Grandpa saw Romer comin up the way, he let out one of those deep belly chuckles. I don't think anyone could fake one of those laughs, I can still hear ol' Grandpa a laughin today.

Romer slid off that ugly horse like he was goin down a Popsicle on a hot day. It was sorta elegant and graceful lookin. Grandpa knew he was in for some excitin times when Romer came around. He looked ev'ry bit the storyteller, what with his worn-out overalls, a long-sleeved shirt and a wide rimmed, sweat-stained felt hat that was molded to his head.

The mornin was still early, so we walked up to the farmhouse and sat on the back porch sippin coffee and talkin. Well, they talked and I just listened, honored to get to sit with the grown-up men-folk. I do believe, however, that I have made up now for all the times that I didn't get to say anythang back then. They got to talkin bout huntin hounds, dogs, bears, wildcats and even deer. I was beginnin to figure this feller must be one of us, only difference was, his horse sure was ugly.

I don't know if it was just cause I was young, but I couldn't help but stare at Romer and he surely had plenty to stare at. He had three big scars on his left cheek and his left hand. The only good fingers he had on that hand was one index finger and his thumb, the other three were missin from the middle knuckle up.

While we sat, Grandpa's redbone coonhound came out from under the porch. She walked right on past me like I wasn't even there and nuzzled up to Romer like she knew him. Right behind her came her little six-month-old pup, Jack, but he stopped at me. Jack, as Grandpa had explained to me, was a redbone and blue tick mix. His daddy is Mr. Scott's blue speckled dog that chases our truck all the way from his house on down to the creek bridge.

As we were enjoyin the early mornin cool and the conversation was flowin, I kept noticin Red's ears perkin up. She kept lookin toward the branch to our north, lettin out an occasional whimper and whine. It wasn't long 'til I could barely hear off in the distance, the faint sound of a hound barkin on the trail of some critter. Then I heard Romer say the hounds were after a "painter." That's when I chimed in and said, "Well, my grandpa is the best house painter around these parts that I know of." After their laughin finally came to a halt, the puzzled look on my face as to what was so funny remained and that's when Grandpa clued me in that a "painter" is country talk for a big cat, like a mountain lion, 'cept they live in the south where we live. Romer told me that Mr. Kent had two calves killed by a panther at his farm not too far up the road. Romer was on the job with his best two hounds, Roscoe and Junior. The hounds I was a hearin had to be them huntin the panther and they sounded like they were headin our way.

Grandpa told me a little bit about Romer and that he was a true woodsman. He went on to say that he was an exterminator of varmints. I could tell Romer wasn't much for braggin on himself and that if I learned anything from him, it would be in the stories he told. Now this fella had as many stories as Grandpa and he could tell I was the one to tell 'em to; he had my full and undivided attention. Romer told of many adventures he and my grandpa had been on. He even told me about the scars on his face that came from the time an ol' black bear had clawed him up. He told me about his missin fingers too, from the time that a huge gator had caught hold of one of his hounds. Romer reached down and took him back, losin some fingers and in the process, nearly losin his arm.

While restin a bit from the story tellin, Romer reached into his pocket, pulled out a big purdy red arrowhead and handed it over to me. It was then that the fascination with Romer turned into a true friendship. He said that arrowhead had come from the Creek Indians. Now, nearly forty years later, I still consider it one of my prized possessions.

I listened to his many stories that October mornin and realized that Romer must know bout ev'rybody round these parts. The value of a varmint exterminator was high to a farmer who might be losin his livestock to predators or his crops to critters. Romer the Exterminator was a celebrity to country folks. He told me he never took pay, but in return for his services of takin out the nuisance animals, the farmers always had a plate set for him at the supper table and a place to lay his head at night. He was known and welcomed all around Florida, Alabama and Georgia. The farmers across the territories that he traveled would also let him tack out the pelts on one side of their barns from the problem critters he killed, so he could sell 'em at the end of the winter season. I could just imagine travelin to new places like Romer did. Me and my trusty sidekick goin on adventures, meetin new people, seein old friends along the way, or for the simple folk, just ramblin through the wilderness after the unknown. I told Romer he was like a mountain man, just without the mountains.

I was in hog heaven with my new friend and my grandpa, talkin and tellin stories. I have always loved to hear good stories, especially my Grandpas. He nicknamed me "Peered-eye," cause when I was listenin to his stories, my big ol' blue eyes would focus as my little mind drank in ev'ry word.

The two hounds were gettin a lot closer trailin after that panther, so close that Red and Jack took off and joined in on the hunt. The trail was warmin up, though the hounds still had plenty of work ahead of them to catch up to the elusive panther. On this still, overcast, cool October day, the sound of the hounds echoed through the tall pines. The dogs were still trailin after the big cat across the ridge goin southwest from Buckhorn Creek and headin toward Goshen Creek. I had never seen a panther before, but I could tell with the coffee drankin and fellowship windin down, I may be gettin my first chance.

Grandpa stopped ev'rythang, looked me right square in the eyes and told me I had to be brave and pay attention to all that goes on once we start in behind these hounds. It could be a couple of hours or a couple of days 'fore we catch up to the panther and there is nothin as sneaky or dangerous as a panther. Grandpa pulled out from under his bed, a sawed off double barrel 16 gauge rabbit eared shotgun and hung it over my shoulder with an old leather strap. All I knew about this gun was that Grandpa had always said it would kick the stew out of a person, but was guaranteed ne'er to miss.

I helped Grandpa get a pack together of flashlights, matches, a coffee pot, a jar of canned smoked mullet, crackers, our jackets and of course, his favorite gun of choice, his prized double barrel muzzle loadin shotgun. We were all ready to go and I had so many butterflies in my belly, I was nearly airborne. Grandma was stayin in town with her sister and I was right glad too, 'cause I knowed Grandpa wouldn't have taken me on such a dangerous hunt had she been home. Just lookin at him now, I could tell he was a bit nervous takin me along anyhow.

Romer picked me up and set me on his ugly horse. I found out then that it wasn't a horse at all; it was a mule, and a girl mule at that. A girl mule is what you would call a "molly." Romer talked to me like I was a grown man, so I made myself sit up straight. He started talkin to his mule like it was a grown man too, I mean woman. He introduced me to Jackie, his girl mule, like she was a person or somethin. I just kinda smiled and told her, "nice to meet you" and she nodded her head like she understood and was glad to meet me too. Just so you know, a mule is the baby of a donkey and horse.

We left the farmhouse and went off towards the sound of the barkin hounds. By the sound of their barkin, I could tell they were gettin closer to the panther cause they were startin to bark a whole lot more. Grandpa and Romer seemed to know exactly where they were goin, them on foot and Jackie totin me on her back, followin without even a lead rope.

I really liked the big mule already. She was surefooted and picked her way along the trail, like I was her responsibility now. I'm glad Jackie takes her job serious-like and she wasn't high strung like a lot of horses. When I was just five years old, I had already fell off a crazy horse and I sure didn't want to do that again.

We worked our way through the hollers, ravines and ridges of tall hickory and white oaks. Those trees were so tall just to look up at them would make your eyes go crossways. As we neared the mouth of Goshen Creek, where it cascades into a big waterfall down into Econfina Creek, the watermelony smell of the water was imprinted into my memory.

Even today, as a grown man, I am still convinced these woods are some of the purdiest I have ever laid eyes on.

While we were waitin, the sound of the hounds seemed to fade, so I asked Romer what we were gonna do. He said we would stay on the trail that the panther was most likely to use while on its way down to the Creek. The big cats almost always would wind up treed or else bayed up in one of the caverns on the side of the creek.

I watched the expressions of the two seasoned woodsmen as they listened to the way the hounds barked while they worked the cat's trail t'wards us. My little mind was drinkin it in through a straw and learnin a bunch. Romer and Grandpa knew the best spot to course the chase, so it was no coincidence that we had a front row seat to the action. We were located at the highest point in the area listenin to the hunt play out. Grandpa said it wouldn't be long now and we would be able to see the chase. The hounds were workin their way down to Goshen Creek and then on past the McQuaig place where the ol' gristmill was. By the way, you can see that very same gristmill down at the Bay County Junior Museum to this day.

At this point, the conversation turned to what we were dealin with and what our plan would be. Romer told me to stay with Jackie no matter what, because that would be the safest place for me. I was instructed to watch her eyes and her ears cause she could sense and detect where the panther was. The slightest sound, movement or smell would alert the ol' girl.

Jackie was bright for a mule and had no fear of even the fiercest animals such as bears, bobcats, snakes, you name it. Unlike a horse, a mule is not a flight animal. When in danger a horse is gonna run, but a mule, especially Jackie, will stand her ground and fight right alongside of you.

As the sunlight was gettin dim, I could hear the sound of the flowin waterfall bein drowned out by the roar of the barkin hounds as they got closer and closer. I was startin to feel queasy and could taste what was left of my moon pie as the thought of this big panther gettin closer put some scary thoughts in my head. Sittin there on the back of the mule, a six-year-old boy in a jacket with a double barrel sawed off shotgun hung across my shoulder, I could smell winter in the light breeze blowin on the high bluff. The memories still flood back about the adventurous night with my Grandpa and my newfound friend, Romer, when I smell the cool night breeze blowin down the Econfina.

I was sure thankin the good Lord for the light of a full moon that night. That meant I wouldn't run down the batteries in my flashlight and I have been known to do that before. I had my night eyes fine-tuned and ready as the hounds were nearin us. In the creek swamp to the south, came the scariest sound I have ever heard. It was a scream that echoed through the ridge and sounded just like a woman screamin at the top of her lungs. Jackie heard it too and held completely still. She laid her ears back, lookin around and workin her nose like a trail dog. All four hounds went silent for just a moment after the panther screamed.

The panther screamed again and it was so loud, I couldn't tell where it was a comin from. Several more light screams followed. Romer then looked at Grandpa and me with concern. He told us that the panther was lettin out the first two for warnin screams, but it was the last light screams that worried him the most. That told him the panther was a momma and was lettin her kittens know to hide in the den cause danger was upon them. The actions of a mother panther are unpredictable and she will stop at nothin to protect her young.

The hounds were barkin every other breath again and they ran straight to where the screams came from; the race heated up! They had to be close to the panther and her young. What a beautiful sound the four hounds made. They were meltin down the woods as they circled within a quarter mile of where we were. They raced back around to where the panther started screamin. Grandpa said that the panther made the big loop tryin to throw the dogs off the trail by goin back across her tracks, another effort fer her to protect her kittens.

I was plum excited to be a witness to the action of the race. Roscoe, Junior, Red and six-month old Jack had to be gettin tired, but they knew this was what they were born to do. What a great job they were doin, too. When they came around the circle the second time, the race and the barkin slowed down just a bit. They were workin right along the ledges and high bluffs of Econfina. A lone dog, ol' Red, began to booger bark just like a yard dog would if he saw a booger. Jack joined in and then the fight was on. For less than a minute, there were some awful sounds, then it ended with a squeal from ol' Red, and then there was silence. Roscoe and Junior started tree barkin and bayin and in just a second, Jack joined in. There was no sound of Red. Roscoe's muffled voice told us they had found the den.

Romer again looked dead at me, told me to stay on Jackie and for no reason was I to get off. We crept slowly across the mouth of Goshen Creek and then along the high bluff lookin over Econfina Creek. Grandpa and Romer were talkin amongst themselves as we began to hear the growlin scream from the panther. The sound was so loud we couldn't pinpoint where she was. The danger was at its highest. Romer was on one side of Jackie, Grandpa on the other and me on her back. This mule was like a canary is to a coal miner as she was tryin to zero in on where the big cat was lurkin. By now, we realized the mother panther was in the trees and the hounds were bayed up at the den. We eased on in to get closer to the dogs. With each step, the dry leaves crackled and crunched under our feet, startin the screamin cat back up again.

I was tremblin so much that Grandpa pulled me off of Jackie's back and all three of us squatted right there in front of her. Grandpa and Romer had their guns up and ready, waitin for the next move. We were between the panther and the cliff.

I heard a slight whimper as Red drug herself over to me and put her muzzle on my knee. She was covered in blood and barely breathin. I reached down to hold her and felt her go limp in my arms. I couldn't fight back the tears from pourin down my freckled cheeks.

Jackie had her radar on; studyin the woods like nothin I've ev'r seen before or since. Then, out of the palmettos behind Jackie, came the panther with no hesitation and in full attack mode. We were all too close to the den with nowhere to go and we were now the hunted. With lightenin speed, the panther, screamin as she came, bolted straight toward us. Before any shots could be fired, the cat was right there. Jackie reacted kickin both back legs in the air with full power, makin contact with the chargin cat. The blow caught the panther and sent her flyin back into the palmettos with a loud thump. Romer and Grandpa flipped on their lights to reveal the dead cat contorted into a lifeless pile. Jackie had killed the panther. A hero mule, who'd a thought?

My heart skipped a few beats on this adventure, I knowed it took a year off my life. On my next birfday, I'd be 8 stead of 7. Romer and his funny lookin horse, better known as Jackie the mule, would be a part of my life for a long time, even to this day.

We tied back the dogs and made camp there for the night. The next mornin, Grandpa and Romer lowered me down the cliff to the mouth of the den where I found two little spotted kittens with their eyes just barely open. I picked both of 'em right up without a fuss and hauled 'em back up in a burlap sack. I asked Romer if we had the right kittens cause these were spotted. He explained to me that the kittens were camouflaged and that the spots would be gone before they were a year old.

The mother of the two kittens was not a mean panther; she was just tryin to feed her young. The problem was that she was killin Mr. Kent's calves to do it and it wound up costin her life. Romer gave me and Grandpa the hide and I still have it today. I made a panther rug that lays right beside my bear rug.

As fer ol' Red, we buried her in the back yard and a fern marks her grave to this day. I don't know why, but still today, that is where the red fern grows. We also kept the two panther kittens at the farm and I got to feed 'em goat's milk. Romer said we were makin more work for him by raisin up them panthers; he told us when they got grown, there was a possibility he'd have to hunt them down, too. They hung around the farm for a couple of years and kept the rabbits thinned down, but they never did mess with the cows. Their visits became less and less until we didn't see them anymore at all. Sometimes, on a cool fall night, I can hear the faint scream of a panther and it still raises the hair on the back of my neck.

At the ripe ol' age of ten, I got my first mule from some of Romer's kinfolk, ol' Leroy Hood, what an interestin man. He bred up some good workin mules from the same horses and donkeys that Jackie came from. I still have one of those ugly horses today, I call em Francis. I'm sure you're a wonderin what happened to Romer. Well, he's still 'round these parts and gettin 'round purdy good for an ol' man. When folks tell me they're havin problems with varmints, I just tell 'em to give Romer a call, he's the Original Exterminator.

If I Don't Do It,
I Ain't Gonna Do It

4 Key Points in Creative Writing

I hope you have enjoyed the stories in this book. I have written the following paragraphs for those of you who are interested in writing or you may have a grandpa that is a hero in overalls and would like to pass his stories on to future generations. Whatever your motivation is, may you find the encouragement and possibly some knowledge in the words below.

Inspiration & Motivation

My inspiration is listed in the very beginning of the book. I have also given a little background on the impact others have had on my life. When you don't really feel like writing, your inspiration will be there to push you along. I've heard of plenty of artists and writers who couldn't produce unless the mood was right. I would not have written this book if the mood always had to be right because more often than not, I didn't feel like writing, but my inspiration pushed me on.

Inspiration alone didn't fuel this engine, it also took motivation. Motivation and determination go hand in hand. Do not put limits on what you can do. Who said you or I couldn't write a book? If somebody else did it, then so can we. Use a motto as a reminder to remain determined to finish. I have a motto and you can use it for free, it's real simple: *If I don't do it, I ain't gonna do it.* Now isn't that a handy dandy motto? Another advantage is that you only have to have one because it can be used for almost anything. Ability can take you so far, throw in some motivation and the sky is the limit!

Imagination

Writing is so wonderful because you can travel and create in your mind a place and a story that you can then share with others who can make it their story. The success of any story will be determined by the writer's ability to capture the attention of the reader. When you describe each word and those words turn into a sentence, then a paragraph, your job is to put feeling, action, and the use of the senses into each word. You may imagine the main character to have black hair, but when you describe the wind blowing each strand and the way it lands on the small of her back, then both you and the reader will imagine her with long hair, although the reader may imagine it blonde. Imagination keeps the storyline the same, but the props are based on the individual reader. Hollywood has taken away this pleasure. There are so many adjectives available, that you, the writer, can make every story engaging. Have fun with it!

Vision

Vision puts organization to your imagination. To have good vision, you must focus on where you are going with what you are writing. It is a good idea to have an outline first, and then fill in the details.

Belief

Inspiration, Motivation, Imagination, Vision, and Belief: These words have many of the same characteristics. At times you will need more belief than you will need vision and more imagination than inspiration, but all will be required at different times during the writing process. Belief begins in you! If you believe that you have something to share with others, then you will. If you believe that you can do something, then you can. Belief can also come from others, which turns into motivation when your belief runs short. The more you write, the more excited you will become and excitement will make your belief much stronger. All you have to do is give life to one idea and then boom, bam, ching, ya got a story!

All stories written or told began with an idea. An idea is what links all 4 key points together. I have written almost every story with just an idea and as I began to write, the story went places I never thought possible. There were even times when I was on the edge of my seat wondering what would happen next!

There are two kinds of people in this world: talkers and doers. My question for you is . . . are you going to just talk about it or are you going to do something about it? I have included blank pages for those of you that are doers. Take your idea (I know you have one) and start fillin' up them pages!

"If I don't do it, I ain't gonna do it."—Scott Kelley

CPSIA information can be obtained at www.ICGtesting.com
Printed in the USA
LVOW121232061211

258017LV00003B/1/P